SOAMES
on the
RANGE

SOAMES
on the
RANGE

Nancy Belgue

Harper*Trophy*Canada™
An imprint of HarperCollins*PublishersLtd*

Soames on the Range
© 2006 by Nancy Belgue. All rights reserved.

Published by Harper*Trophy*Canada™, an imprint of HarperCollins
Publishers Ltd

Harper*Trophy*Canada™ is a trademark of HarperCollins Publishers.

First edition

HarperCollins books may be purchased for educational, business, or
sales promotional use through our Special Markets Department.

HarperCollins Publishers Ltd
2 Bloor Street East, 20th Floor
Toronto, Ontario, Canada
M4W 1A8

www.harpercollins.ca

Library and Archives Canada Cataloguing in Publication

Belgue, Nancy, 1951–
Soames on the range / Nancy Belgue. – 1st ed.

ISBN-13: 978-0-00-200768-9
ISBN-10: 0-00-200768-1

I. Title.

PS8553.E4427S62 2007   JC813'.6   C2006-905832-6

HC 9 8 7 6 5 4 3 2 1

The author wishes to acknowledge the support of the Canada
Council for the Arts.

Printed and bound in the United States
Set in Nofret
Text design by Sharon Kish

To Terry

1

It was a family meeting with a real twist. My mother sat on the edge of her seat, legs crossed, flipping her foot up and down. My sisters, India and Paris, ten-year-old twins, slouched in a loveseat by the window, bookends with bad posture.

My father stood in the centre of the room, hands on hips, looking uncharacteristically bleary eyed and unshaven.

Have I mentioned we never have family meetings at my house?

We are not, I should add, the most normal family you've ever met. Family meetings are just way too Disney for us. Usually we communicate by shouting.

My name, for the record, is San Francisco Soames. Named after the city. Paris is named after a city too. India got an entire country. These are places my parents travelled to when they were young and in love.

Which they aren't any more. Which brings me back to the family meeting.

"I'm moving out," my father said. He started to pace, as if a moving target would be harder to miss.

It wasn't really a surprise. They hadn't been getting along for years, or so it seemed to me. India and Paris slid farther down into the cushions of the loveseat. They have very red hair and freckles. But they are not as sweet as they look.

Mom, whose name is Delta, pulled at a loose thread on her macramé belt. She works in the library, but her heart is in a commune somewhere in North Dakota.

India asked, "Where are you going?"

And here's where things took a real turn for the worse.

"I'm moving in with Ralph," my father said.

"Ralph?" Paris repeated.

"Ralph Brewster," my mother said, speaking for the first time.

"Angela's father?" Paris asked.

"Yes," Rocky said. Rocky is my father's name. He changed it when he was fifteen, the same age I am now. He said he liked the movie. I thought he meant the one about the boxer, but it was really *The Rocky Horror Picture Show* he was talking about. His real name is Alfred, but he denies it if anyone asks him.

"Is Mr. Brewster moving out too?" India asked.

Rocky stopped and looked to Delta for help. She shook her head.

"We're moving in together," Rocky said, a significant tone to his voice. Delta looked out the window.

Paris and India glanced at each other but didn't seem to be getting it.

I, unfortunately, understood.

"We're going to be living as a *couple*," Rocky said.

"You mean you're gay?" Paris asked.

I squirmed in my seat. I wished I were anywhere but where I was.

Rocky had the grace to blush a little. He drew up a foot-stool and sat forward in this very intense way he has when he's teaching us about something. Rocky used to be a teacher, after all. Now he's a guidance counsellor. In my high school.

Paris and India inched backwards in their seats. Delta stood up and placed a hand on each twin's shoulder. I decided I'd leave. There are some father–son conversations you just don't want to have.

It was the middle of November and the backyard was still covered with leaves, mainly because I hadn't bothered raking them for a month or so. We live in Vermont and the leaves are a very big tourist attraction, so it's kind of hard to resent the hell out of them—but I do. Sometimes I make them into a bonfire even though it's against the law. Delta freaks and tells me to compost them, but there're just too many.

The screen door squeaked behind me. Delta was on the back porch, her arms wrapped around herself, her hair blowing in the wind.

"Snow in the air," she called to me.

"So how long have you known about this?" I asked. I bent and picked up the rake and had to stop myself from hurling it at the house.

"I found out about Ralph a few months ago." She scuffed her way through the blowing leaves. The tree branches were bare now. She might be right, I thought. It could snow.

She was beside me, looking at me with concerned eyes. Her face was older than it had seemed before the family meeting. Or maybe I was looking at her more carefully. The lines around her eyes didn't go away when she stopped smiling and the skin around her jaw jiggled a bit when she opened her mouth to speak.

"I thought something was wrong for a lot longer than that, though. I just didn't know what."

Paris and India were on the porch now as if fleeing from Rocky. Delta started back to the house. "Are you okay?" she asked over her shoulder.

I gripped the rake until my hands hurt, then started pushing the leaves into piles. I didn't know what else to do.

Delta sighed, grabbed each twin by a hand, and went inside again. Rocky talked to her in the kitchen—I could see them through the window, standing together, like old times. I swallowed a lump in my throat.

Rocky came out on the porch next. I shoved the leaves into a giant pile and thought about crawling inside. I didn't want him to speak to me.

"Cisco," he said. He walked across the lawn toward me.

I used to wish my father was like other fathers. He never quite fit in, you know? He tried coaching Little League, but didn't really understand baseball. I spent more time worrying about him saying something weird, like the time he started lecturing the team about the merits of cotton vs polyester, for God's sake, than I did watching the ball.

"I want to talk to you," he said.

Delta was watching from the window. Rocky took a step toward me. I'm not sure how he thought I'd react. I don't usually let my emotions run away with me, but that day a black anger erupted and I couldn't see anything except explosions of light rocketing across my brain.

"Are you okay?" Rocky asked. His voice sounded hollow.

I just left. Left him standing there among the piles of leaves, holding his hand out.

The downtown of Lovell is not much more than a crossroads. Population: 3,000. I've lived here all my life and everyone knows me. I know everyone too. Most of the time this is just a pain in the ass, but today it was a major problem. I wondered who already knew about Rocky's secret. The possibilities were virtually endless, like the combinations in a Rubik's Cube. I passed the bowling lanes and the Pump Restaurant. The *P* was burnt out and someone had scrawled an *H* in neon spray paint over the lifeless bulbs. Farther down the street, a few strings of Christmas lights blinked anemically in the grey afternoon light. Sundays in small towns are why people go postal.

I passed Mill Street, where the Brewsters live. I wondered if they were having a family meeting too. It was tempting to walk on over and see how Mr. Brewster was breaking the news to *his* family. He had two children, Angela and Sharon, big pudgy girls with pin-heads on oversized bodies. Sharon was in my class at high school. Angela was the same age as the twins. I remembered Mrs. Brewster from the lineups at the ballpark concession. Mona was a sloppy woman who refused to get a job. She wore her hair in a jet-black mullet, smoked menthol cigarettes and ordered pizza every Friday night. I know, because I work weekends in the pizza parlour and I always take her order. "Two large pizzas, triple cheese," she'll say in an exhausted tone. "To give me a break from cooking," she'll add, expecting sympathy no doubt for all the cans she's opened during the week.

Mr. Brewster runs a ski hill over near Stowe, so I figured Rocky'd probably be moving there. I'd been there a few times, to stay in the chalet where Mr. Brewster lived. He commuted there from Lovell, but hadn't been seen much lately. I remembered he had jars of peanut butter in the cupboard, and nothing else. He was skinny and twitchy, and had a constant tan. Did Rocky really think anyone was going to be understanding about this?

I hunched my shoulders against the wind and sat on the bank of the Huntington River. A few lonely ducks were still hanging around. Most of the others had gone south over a month ago.

I tried to think about what school was going to be like tomorrow, but didn't have the guts. I had the imagination, though, and all I knew was I didn't want to go. The kids in this town aren't exactly tolerant. You'd think they would be, since lots of the parents are like Rocky and Delta, right out of the Summer of Love, but there is a vocal group of yahoos and rednecks too. And, this town being no different than most small towns, the rednecks and yahoos have worked their way to the top of the food chain. It's not cool here to do well in school. It's not cool to like art. And it's definitely not cool to have a gay father. Especially a gay father who is the guidance counsellor. I cringed.

There were other things I had to think about. Things like how the twins were going to get along. They were known around town as the Red Scourge because they have this unbe-lievable red hair. But they are fractious little beasts too. Hardly a week goes by that Delta doesn't have to go into the school and haul one or the other of them home because they've been in trouble "with the law," as Paris sarcastically puts it. They are scofflaws, my mom says. And she says it fondly, like it's some-thing to be proud of. I think she sees it as a holdover from her bra–burning, consciousness raising, hippie idealism.

Problem is, the twins don't need her egging them on. One of these days, they're going to get into some real trouble. And then all her crazy ideas are going to be cold comfort. My grandmother tells me I worry too much, but this family needs serious taking care of. The twins have incredibly high IQs, somewhere around 130, making them borderline geniuses. It seems to me that they need to have this mental horsepower channelled into something a little bit more productive than thinking up ways to defy society. But hey, I come from a gene pool that reveres Ralph Nader, Malcolm X and Susan Sarandon. I can only do so much.

I shoved the thought of the twins out of my mind. Let them take care of themselves, for once. I was the one who was going to have to face Tommy Lee Lester, Francis O'Reilly and their miniature henchman Jason Lonigan.

It was probably the cold, but I couldn't stop shivering.

The waters of the Huntington River kept flowing. Black as pitch and twice as thick. Dunkin' Donuts coffee cups and an old tire churned by. I remembered coming here in grade one and playing Pooh sticks on the stone bridge. Idly, I picked up a branch with a few brown leaves still attached and tossed it into the foaming white caps. The stick spun around—like a body on those amusement-park rides that use centrifugal force to pin you to the outside of the cage—then shot into the vortex, its spindly leaves waving a forlorn farewell.

2

Sing Sing. That's the affectionate term for Lovell District High School. Not-so-affectionate terms are the Projects, the canal (after Love Canal) and the Lockup. Not very original, but certainly descriptive. Ever since Columbine, kids have taken a dim view of school. A few try to carry on the peppy traditions, like cheerleading and school sports, but most of us just put in our time and go home. I hate to think school's any kind of preparation for life, but there you are.

Today, Monday morning, the low-slung, 1950s concrete building looked even less inviting than usual. The no-frills signage announced Parents' Night was coming. I couldn't have been more thrilled. The school lobby is decorated with murals that kids have painted over the years. I contributed this year, with a truly outstanding piece of graffiti art, if I do say so myself. I stayed after school for three weeks, working with subdued shades of grey and black. The final picture shows the band playing with sticks, cans and bean-shakers while the football team scrimmages for a sack of money. I mean, someone had to make a statement when the band's budget was eliminated so the athletic teams could get new uniforms. I got hauled on the carpet for that one, and figure it's just a matter of time before they paint over it. The newspaper came out and did a story on my picture, made me into a local crusader for freedom of speech. Kinda made it hard for the administration to shut it down. I tagged it tuba(d)4U in interlocking bubble-letters. A real masterpiece. Painting that mural was the best part of coming to school.

"Hey, Freak!" someone yelled, and at least ten kids looked up from their combination locks. It took a minute before they realized that this particular freak was me. Nine heads ducked back down behind their locker doors, relieved. It was starting already, I thought.

But it was only Jason Lonigan, displaying his usual lack of finesse in the humour department.

"Hey, Freak," he said again. Jason is a hanger-on. He follows Tommy Lee Lester and Francis O'Reilly around like the quacking duck pull-toy my sisters had when they were toddlers.

"Lonigan," I said. I scanned the hall. Trouble with Lonigan is that he's usually not far from Lester or O'Reilly. But today, the other two were nowhere around. "S'up?" I said, looking into his red-rimmed eyes.

"You heard the news?"

I shook my head. I have to say, my usual bully radar can't have been working at full capacity because I walked right into what happened next.

"No." I stacked my books under my arm.

"One of the faculty's a faggot. Heard he jumped out of the closet over the weekend." His lip curled in a sneer. "Got any idea who that might be?"

I shut my locker and spun the combination dial on my lock. I was buying time, I guess, trying to think of a snappy retort. Mostly, though, I just felt weary. I could see a long, hard day ahead of me.

Lonigan strutted around in front of me. He wasn't going to let his big moment pass.

I sighed. "Give it a rest, Lonigan." I sidestepped him. Lonigan's only about five foot four, so he tends to be tenacious to make up for his size. I'm already six feet, but totally unintimidating.

"Oh yeah?" he demanded. "Oh YEAH?"

"Now, that's intelligent," I said. "Oh yeah?"

The expression in Lonigan's eyes changed. He was getting confused and I knew things would go one of two ways, neither of which appealed to me. He'd either start swearing or he'd start pushing.

"Lonigan! Soames!" Mr. Vasco appeared at the end of the hall. "Get to class. I'm watching you!"

"Later, wuss baby," Lonigan hissed.

"Wuss baby?" I said.

"Shut up!"

"Wuss baby?" I repeated. A smile grabbed my mouth and tugged it. "Wuss—"

That's when he punched me. The force of the blow spun me around and the next thing I knew, he'd launched himself into the air and fastened himself to my back. It was like trying to dislodge a tick that has embedded its pincers into your flesh.

Doors opened along the hallway, teachers spilled out of their classrooms, and Mr. Vasco barrelled down the hall like a Scud missile. It took three teachers to pull Lonigan off me. I watched as he got dragged to the office. A puddle of blood formed at my feet. My nose was gushing like a garden hose. Mrs. Harper told me to tilt my head back. She handed me a wad of tissues and before the blood had even begun to clot,

I was sitting in the Principal's Office staring at Lonigan, while Mr. Shipton delivered ultimatums and talked about "suspensions" and "zero tolerance" through clenched jaws.

My dad knocked on the door and Mr. Shipton motioned for him to come in. Lonigan's mother was on her way from the dry cleaner, where she worked as a presser. She pushed her way into the room without knocking, smelling hot and steamy like a freshly pressed shirt. She was under five feet and I had the crazy idea that it looked like a war of tall people against short people. She glared at us as if my father was a tall Satan and I was the devil's gawky spawn. Lonigan and his mother resemble each other in ways aside from their height. For one thing, she's as pugnacious as he is. This thought gave me an uncomfortable moment. Here was I, stacking Lonigan's behaviour up against his gene pool. What if people did the same with me and my dad? I mean, ever since I was three years old, I'd heard the comments. I've been called everything from Rocky II to Chip off the old Rock by just about everyone who's ever met us.

"I suppose he's going to get off just because his father's a teacher here," she began before Mr. Shipton even said hello.

She glared at me with all of Lonigan's pink-eyed fury. The two of them reminded me of lab rats.

"The school's policy on fighting is very clear, Mrs. Lonigan," said Mr. Shipton. He gestured at a seat, but Mrs. Lonigan remained standing. She put both hands on the principal's desk and leaned into his face.

"And that is?" she asked.

Mr. Shipton sat back slightly. "Everyone involved gets a week suspension. Period. No exceptions."

Mrs. Lonigan slapped the desk with her open palm. The sound reverberated through the office like a firecracker in a metal garbage pail. Even Jason jumped in terror.

"Not going to happen," she growled at the principal's startled face.

"Mrs. Lonigan," Mr. Shipton began before she could cut him off.

"Not. Going. To. Happen." She pushed herself off the desk and whirled to stare down her son. "Jason!" He snapped to attention. "Get your books. We will be taking this matter to the superintendent," she snarled at Mr. Shipton, but she was staring at my father as if he'd just crawled out from under a rock.

"Heard you moved in with Ralph Brewster over the weekend," she said, finally sticking it to Rocky. "My cousin works over at that ski hill, told me all about your little love nest."

So that was how Lonigan knew. I slumped into my chair, examining the floor, thinking how nice it would be to disappear. I heard Rocky move toward the window, as if he might jump out. I glanced up. His face was the colour of ashes.

Pleased with the effect she was having, Mrs. Lonigan surveyed her audience, then picked up steam. "Now that you've finally owned up to what you are, you're looking to make trouble for decent people like my son," she hissed at my father. "You ever think of the example you're setting for the kids in this school?"

"Mrs. Lonigan—" Rocky began.

She cut him off and turned to me. "And you!" she said, pointing, her eyes flinty.

I could see her mind cranking away, looking for some way to put the blocks to me. A light went on, you could actually see it happen. She allowed herself a righteous smile.

"Propositioning my boy! Just like the old man."

There it was. The famous phrase. *Just like the old man.*

Confusion settled on Lonigan's face. He watched his mother

like a deaf person reading lips, trying to figure out if he'd understood correctly. She grabbed his arm and pulled him to the door.

"No kid should have to put up with that kind of harassment," she shrieked when she got Lonigan between her and the door.

I could see Jason ducking his head, letting her take the lead, sensing he was about to get a reprieve.

"Cisco?" Mr. Shipton said, turning to me. "What's Mrs. Lonigan talking about?"

"Nothing!" I said. I turned and looked at Mrs. Lonigan's face. "I have no idea what she's talking about!" I didn't, either.

"Oh yeah?" Mrs. Lonigan took two steps forward. Her anger sputtered out of her mouth in short, choppy sentences. "You homo. Jason told me all about you. How you hang out with girls. Make fun of him. Put him down. Spend all your time in the home-ec room. Good place for a homo, if you ask me. Making cookies! Jason told me, don't you think he didn't. Even before your old man took the plunge, Jason'd told me all about you. How you watch him. Touch him in gym class. Say things! Soon's I got the call this morning, I knew what'd happened. You came on to him once too often. You and your snotty, I'm-better-than-you attitude. Then you grabbed him. I know all about how it happened. Giving him the eye, rubbing up against him. My boy's just trying to swat off an unwanted fly, that's all. Can't blame him. You suspend my boy and the whole town's going to hear about this." She finally gasped to a halt.

The only thing that resembled truth in her remarks was the fact that I did like to bake cookies. If I hadn't been so pissed off, I'd have had to admire her creativity. Trouble is, once something like that is out there, it has a life of its own. You get to spend the next part of your life proving it isn't true. An interesting thought occurred to me: How is it that Lonigan's family never had to prove basic intelligence?

Mr. Shipton came out from behind his desk. "You're making a lot of accusations without any proof, Mrs. Lonigan," he said. "You'd best be careful."

"Careful! It's just like I said it would be. You're going to stick up for one of your own, never mind the bad influence people like that have on the rest of us. Come on, Jason!" She elbowed Lonigan through the door. The confusion had cleared from his face. In its place were equal parts shame and triumph. His mother slammed the door behind her. I could see them out the window when they appeared in the parking lot, and she was still talking, gesturing with both hands and giving Jason an occasional shove.

My father sank into a seat. Mr. Shipton and I remained standing.

"Brother," said Mr. Shipton to no one in particular.

"Now what?" my father said.

Mr. Shipton glanced at me. "The suspension stands, Cisco. I'm sorry, but that's the policy. A week."

"What about Lonigan?" I asked.

"Same thing." Mr. Shipton ran his hands through his hair.

"You mean his mother gets to shout all those lies and nothing happens?" I asked.

Shipton shook his head like he didn't quite know what to say. "Cisco, would you excuse us, please. I need to talk to your father alone."

"You go get your books, then go on home, son," Rocky said. He hunched forward, staring at his feet.

"Great!" I said. "I get attacked because of something *you* did, they get to make up all those lies about me and then I get suspended. That's just great!"

"Cisco!" my father said.

Mr. Shipton glanced away, embarrassed.

I bolted from the office, ignoring the curious stare of Mrs. Proulx, the school secretary, and left the building. Screw the books. A suspension meant I'd lose my chance to audition for the school play. Plus, I'd miss the annual trip to NYC to see the Museum of Modern Art, something I'd been waiting for since eighth grade!

The driveway was empty when I got home. It was Delta's day to do kids' programming at the library. Part of me was glad she wasn't there. I didn't want to answer any of her questions about what happened. The other part of me, the not-so-nice part, was pissed. Now I didn't have anyone to take my anger out on. I'd forgotten my key again, so I climbed in the kitchen window like I usually do. The house was nice like this, all peaceful. I almost never get to be home alone. There's always the TV blaring some dumb kids' show or video. The twins own everything the Olsens have ever done, God help us all. Or else Delta's listening to the Grateful Dead. Or Rocky's playing a Queen CD. Then there's the constant ringing of the phone. Delta works on about a thousand different committees, and the girls know everyone in Lovell. When I was twelve, I tried padding my room to keep out the noise, but the twins kept busting in and asking me questions about everything from sex to bare-knuckles boxing, so I concluded that Delta, as usual, wasn't paying much attention to what was happening. I needed to hear what was going on. So I gave up.

I opened the fridge, but there was nothing to eat except last night's leftovers—tofu noodle casserole. The kitchen smelled of garlic and mouldy cheese. I shoved Delta's jar of Café Libre aside and found the coffee I kept hidden in the back of the cupboard, put on a pot and plunked myself down at the kitchen table. Any second now, I expected Rocky to show up. I poured myself some coffee and sat and waited. He would arrive, breathless from riding his bike all the way from the high school. He'd be red faced, because he's not in as great shape as he used to be. His hair would stick up in all directions. The pot–belly that he has developed over the past few years would strain at the faded blue denim shirt he always wore.

The clock on the wall is a big one with a second hand that clicks each time it moves. I hate it. As a kid I liked to unplug it because then Delta would miss one of her meetings and stay home with us.

"Silly boy," Delta always said when she moved the butcher block aside to discover the plug hanging free. "Mommy's got a committee, my little cheroots," she'd say as she stuffed her raffia bag full of agendas printed on recycled paper.

I sighed. I contemplated whipping myself up an omelette with free–range eggs. Maybe a soufflé. I was reviewing the possibilities presented by the mouldy cheese when I was seized by an urge stronger than good sense. I picked up the kitchen shears and severed the clock cord at the point where it emerged from the giant black–and–white face. The second hand stopped with a satisfying last *click*. The silence in the kitchen was complete.

3

I must have fallen asleep. Rocky wasn't home. Neither was Delta. Nor were the twins. It was as if cutting the clock cord had frozen everyone in time. The kitchen clock was the only clock in the house and now I had no idea what time it was.

Why hadn't Rocky come home after me?

I flicked on the TV screen and surfed around until I hit CNN. The time was displayed in the lower corner. Three–thirty. Sleep is an escape, they say, and I'd just escaped for four and a half hours. Where *was* everybody? Delta should have been home by now. The silence in the house felt all wrong.

A few kids straggled home from school. I recognized Merrilee Pravda who lived across the square. She was with Lionel Costello. They pretend they are boyfriend and girl-friend because nobody ever asks either of them out. The only time I'd ever watched the homeward migration of the school kids was when I was sick, and I hadn't paid much atten-tion except to think how lucky I was not being one of them.

Knowing that today I was an outcast, a suspended student, gave the whole parade an entirely different allure.

Merrilee and Lionel were talking. I had never noticed before, but she motor-mouthed faster than the ill-tempered jays that perch on the spruce tree out back. Lionel smiled and nodded, his spiky black hair razoring the air. They passed without glancing my way, and I wondered if maybe word hadn't gotten around about the suspension.

But no.

The next ones down my street were Tommy Lee Lester and Francis O'Reilly.

Lovell has five distinct neighbourhoods. There's the town square, where the big houses are, the houses that predate the Revolution, the houses the tourist wives point at with the same desire their husbands no doubt felt when they got their first copy of *Playboy*. That's the right side of town. There's also the River Road development. The newer houses are built there, and it's where most of the professionals who work in Burlington live. They have gates and alarm systems. Then there's the old town. Big, century-old houses, big shade trees, big yards. But not much money. The arts community likes this area. Guess where I live.

Then there's the wrong side of town, which kind of blends with the fifth neighbourhood: the country. The wrong side has scary little bungalows, mobile homes and lawns seeded with a mishmash of car parts, busted kids' toys and treed with empty, unused clotheslines. These homes, crammed together on small lots, flow out into the country in a widening river of rusty boat trailers, wooden windmills, tree stumps and satellite dishes. Tommy Lee Lester and Francis O'Reilly bus in from the country every day, so there could be only one reason they were loitering outside my house.

I ducked behind the lace curtains, knowing they didn't hide

a thing. The movement caught Lester's eye and he nudged O'Reilly in the ribs. What were they planning to do? Because unless they had a battering ram, they were going to be disappointed. I wasn't planning on leaving the house anytime in the next century.

The twins turned the corner just then and headed toward home. Lester shoved off from the fence he was leaning against and muttered something to O'Reilly. I could read his lips, having studied how this is done during my Helen Keller phase. Oh, I realize she was blind and didn't read lips, but Rocky told me to stop crashing into the furniture and open my goddamn eyes. No one seemed to miss the sound of my voice, so the deaf-mute part went on much longer. After a month or so, Delta took me to a psychiatrist, who asked me what the hell I thought I was doing, said that I was not Helen Keller, had the good fortune to have all my senses in fine working order and that I should just cut it out, for Christ's sake and save my mother a boatload of money. He then dragged deeply on his cigarette and stared at me with a challenge in his eyes. He scared the shit out of me. Shrinks aren't supposed to talk like that, I muttered, forgetting my muteness, studying what looked like blood under his fingernails. He squinted into the smoke and stabbed the glowing tip of the cigarette at me for emphasis. "You ain't seen nothin' yet," he suggested in a grim monotone. "We're just getting started here, son."

Delta was thrilled with my rapid recovery. It wasn't until last year that I found out my "therapist" was a disbarred psychiatrist who'd started a new career as a butcher in the Piggly Wiggly, but since Delta felt sorry for him she'd entrusted my delicate psychological condition to a man who now butterflied pork chops for a living.

The twins were running now, their heads bobbing on their gawky little bodies like those Chinese lanterns you see growing in the garden this time of year. Even from my lace-covered sanctuary I could see Lester's eyes light up. He and O'Reilly started to walk toward them. I clenched the curtains in my sweaty palms. They wouldn't hurt two little girls, would they?

I couldn't see anything. The twins were blocked by Lester and O'Reilly's simian shoulders. No one else was on the street; it was as if the whole town except my sisters and the baboon brothers had been sucked up a giant tube into a hovering spaceship. I was going to have to rescue my sisters.

The cold November air hit me in the face as I stepped out onto the porch. A wind came up. The grass rippled across the lawns like a wave in a stadium full of spectators. I thought of the Romans feeding early Christians to the lions. The fluting voices of my sisters reached my ears. I filled my lungs and started down the walk. Paris spotted me and waved.

I stopped. Things seemed to be under control. Perhaps my intervention wasn't needed. O'Reilly turned. His eyes glittered. Lester gave India a small pat on the head. She looked at him as if he were from another planet. The girls stepped around the lunkheads and skipped in my direction.

"You got suspended," Paris trilled. "How cool!"

"News travels fast," I said, glancing at O'Reilly, who was moving toward us.

"What'dja do?" India asked.

"Later." I pushed them toward the porch.

They twirled and saw Lester and O'Reilly slinking up the walk.

They stood their ground, one twin on each side of me. Paris put her warm small hand in my very cold one.

"Oh, look, how cute!" Lester sneered.

"Got yourself a security team, eh, Soames?"

"Beat it, kids," said Lester.

India took my other hand.

Lester and O'Reilly stood there uncertainly. Paris picked up a lump of dirt from the grass and heaved it at them. It hit Lester on the shoulder with a satisfying squishy splat.

"That's dogshit!" he screamed, looking at his T-shirt as if it had grown fangs.

"Run!" yelled Paris.

I was yanked backwards as the twins dragged me up the porch.

"You little . . ."

India pushed me inside and slammed the door behind the three of us. O'Reilly's face appeared in the small window, right above Delta's homemade wreath of battered pine cones. He was foaming at the mouth.

The street suddenly came to life. Mrs. Franks' door opened and her Rottweiler, Honey, of the dogshit hand-grenade, gambolled across the street ready to make a new deposit. She stopped at the edge of our lawn and sniffed the air suspiciously. Her tail slowed. A car engine fired to life. The paper boy studded lawns with the afternoon edition of the *Burlington Star*. Delta's Beetle rounded the corner, coming our way.

Lester called to O'Reilly, "Leave it."

O'Reilly headed for the sidewalk, but not until he'd picked up another lump of poop and fired it at the window, where it smeared into a wet brown Rorschach blot that reminded me of my one and only session with the butcher-psychiatrist.

"What d'you see here, kid?" he'd asked, shoving an ink blot at me.

"A flower?" I'd suggested, playing along.

"What you see here, kid," he'd said, leaning back in a squeaky swivel chair and looking down his nose at me, "is nothing but bullshit."

Right on, I thought, staring at the brownly glistening window. Right on.

4

"Those boys do not have pleasant auras," Delta said as she clumped up the stairs.

"They were going to kill Cisco," Paris shouted dramatically from the powder room, where she was scrubbing dogshit off her hands.

"What happened to the clock?" India yelled from the kitchen.

I crossed my arms and sat on the stairs.

Delta gave me a look and headed down the hall to the kitchen. "Cisco," she shouted back, "what have you got against this clock?"

"I got suspended today," I told her. I followed her and was now leaning against the door.

She turned. India peered at me from behind her glass of soymilk and fistful of carob cookies.

"Why?"

"Fighting."

Delta expended her breath with an audible *whoosh* and collapsed at the rickety table.

"You know I don't condone violence."

"Yeah, well, maybe you should be telling that to Jason Lonigan and not me."

Her eyes flashed. "Jason Lonigan?"

Jason and the lunkheads had been hounding me since grade school. They'd always had it in for me and my family. Delta knew this. She'd had endless meetings with parents and teachers over the years. All about how "poor" Cisco couldn't make friends.

"Yep."

"Are you hurt?" For the first time she noticed the crusted blood on the inside of my nostrils and the slight swelling on the bridge of my nose. She started toward me.

I backed up.

"No." I didn't want her to touch me. I wanted her to touch me. I didn't know what I wanted her to do.

She kept on coming, though. And before I could back up any farther, she had grabbed me and was hugging me with surprising force. It took a minute before I realized she was crying.

I patted her back, confused.

The twins stared at us, chewing suspended. We'd never seen Delta cry. Ever.

"Hey, Mom," I said. "It's okay." Pat, pat.

At my use of the word *mom*, she cried even harder. My shoulder was damp. The twins started to wail. I was sur-rounded by weeping women. My eyes misted over.

"I'm sorry, Cisco," Delta hiccuped into my shoulder. "Let me look at you."

She pulled back and gingerly touched my nose. Tears swelled in her eyes again and she sniffed, loudly. "You poor boy," she muttered.

"Yeah, well . . ."

"What did Rocky have to say about this?" she asked, starting to get angry.

"So far, I haven't seen him," I said. This was beginning to
really piss me off too. The least he could have done was give
me a call.

"What time did all this happen?"

"Right before first period."

Her eyes widened. "You mean you've been here alone since
this morning?" She glanced at the clock and remembered it
was stuck at 10:30. Checked her wristwatch. "Six hours?"

Had it been six hours? There really was something to be
said for cutting the clock.

Delta marched to the phone. "Where's that number?" she
muttered as she rummaged through the mess on the phone
table. "Son of a bitch."

The twins and I exchanged shocked glances. First crying,
now profanity.

"Rocky!" she shouted into the receiver. "Why aren't you
over here?"

I took off out into the yard. I guess part of me had rational-
ized his not coming after me by thinking he'd been caught up
at school. Now, here was Delta, talking to him on his new home
number. How long he'd been there and why he hadn't come to
see me were two questions I didn't really want answered. The
afternoon light had gone weak and watery the way it does in
November, a sure sign of snow. When I was a kid, I loved the first
snowfall. It was late this year. Somehow all it made me think of
was the start of the ski season, and how Rocky was going to be
living in a chalet on the outskirts of Stowe with Ralph Brewster.
Probably wearing mukluks or some other creepy après-ski gear.
Working on a permanent tan, getting his teeth whitened.

"Cisco," called Delta from the back porch, "Rocky wants to
talk to you."

I thought about it for a moment and shook my head.

"You sure?"

"Gotta go," I said, heading for the street.

"Cisco!" Delta shouted after me.

The frigid air made my nose ache. An old black dog started following me, slinking along like some sort of malevolent spirit. I knew a kid who went nuts once and thought he was a dog. He used to sit in the town square barking at people. Ronnie, his name was, and he finally got taken away somewhere. His mother still lived in town, with five or six other kids. There was no sign of Ronnie, though. I hadn't thought of him for years.

I realized I was heading to Karen's house. Karen and I worked together at the Pizza Oven on weekends. I liked her. She was a year older than I was and lived in Lovell's only apartment building. She probably had fifteen tattoos, although I hadn't actually counted. Her hair was dyed in two tones, red and white. She lived with her father and two younger brothers. Her mother died when she was ten.

The apartment building was only two stories high and Karen's family lived on the ground floor at the corner. There were a couple of kids' bikes parked outside, one of Karen's fantastical tree-stump sculptures and a flowerpot with a rosemary bush that I'd given her, still growing despite the cold weather. I'd have to remind her to take it inside for the winter. Karen was sitting in the window talking on the phone. She waved when she spotted me.

"Hey, Cisco!" she called, opening the window. "Don't you know it's 32 degrees out there?"

I'd left without putting on a coat and my nose was aching.

"Come in, Bonehead," she yelled.

I clambered over the mountains of stuff piled on her skinny concrete patio and let myself in the sliding door.

The smell of onions and garlic filled the room.

"Yo, Cisco," Karen said, padding into the living room trailing the phone cord behind her. Karen's the only person I know who doesn't have a portable phone. "Take your chains off. Set a spell."

I ignored her and wandered into the kitchen, raised the lid on the pot and stirred its contents, trying to figure out what she was cooking. Karen's many things, including a totally original artist, but a good cook isn't one of them. I chucked a handful of spices into the pot of what looked like stew.

"Just in time," she said. "Serious food abuse going on in here."

"Karen," I muttered, rummaging around in the pantry, "I can't keep staging these interventions. You've got to learn some basic skills. Your family depends on it."

Karen rolled her eyes. "Why learn when I've got you? What happened to your nose?"

"Got punched out in school."

"No way." She leaned in for a better look.

"You never should have dropped out. You could have pro-tected me."

"So who did it? No, let me guess. Tommy Lee?"

"Nope."

"Had to be O'Reilly, then."

"Nope. Lonigan."

"Lonigan! That midget? He hardly comes to your armpit."

"Yeah, well he's small but quick."

"Come on, Cisco. Tell me what happened."

She settled herself on a kitchen chair, eyes shining.

"Well, in the first place he attacked me."

"Goes without saying."

I glanced at her.

"You casting aspersions on my manhood?"

"Nah, you'd just rather bake than fight."

"Don't spread it around, okay?"

"Geez, Cisco, lighten up. You're not the first kid to come home with a bloody nose, you know. Probably do your image some good."

"Just what is that supposed to mean?" I studied her with narrowed eyes through the steam rising from the simmering pot.

"Can I be frank?" She didn't wait for the answer. "You know how some of the kids tease you about stuff."

She was talking about the fact that I hated sports, liked art and cooking. "Yeah, so?"

"So, this will probab'ly shake 'em up some. You hit him back?"

"Karen, this is a whole new side of you." I pretended astonishment. Her reaction surprised me. I was looking for a little comfort, after all. "What did you think I should have done?"

She shrugged. "Decked him?"

We stared at each other. I saw myself spinning around trying to dislodge Lonigan from my back. I felt the pressure on my windpipe as he tightened his arm against my throat and the sting of his knuckles as they connected with my nose.

"Rocky's gay," I said.

Her eyes widened. "No shit?"

"No shit."

"So how did you find out?"

"He told us yesterday. He's discovered his true self, he's moving out. He's got a boyfriend."

"That why Lonigan jumped you?"

"Yeah, I guess."

"Hey, I shouldn't of said anything about all that other stuff. I'm sorry."

I stood there, wooden spoon dripping Karen's watery gravy onto the grimy stove.

"It's just that—" she stopped.

I raised an eyebrow.

"Never mind."

"What?" I said.

"How come you let those guys bug you all the time? Lonigan and the thugs? Why don't you ever just tell them to take a hike? Pop 'em in the eye or something?"

Karen had always been a fighter, had always been ready to right the wrongs of the world. All through school, even before we'd gotten to be friends, she regularly got hauled into the office because she'd bloodied the nose of one bully or another. Like the time when she was in fourth grade and I was in third grade and she rubbed Lonigan's face in red paint to pay him back for stealing my bike. She was looking at me now, hard. Studying me till I squirmed.

"Why should I? I don't believe in violence."

Karen barked a bitter kind of laugh. "A swift kick to the wazoo is the only thing jerks like that understand." She jabbed a right at my chin, making me jump back a step or two. "So, you just going to take it?"

"Take what?" I was getting confused now. "The suspension?"

"No. All the crap Lonigan's going to dish out."

I was beginning to wonder if Karen had Mr. Shipton's office wired. I wouldn't put it past her.

"What do you mean?"

"Oh, come on, Cisco. Those idiots have been after you for years, always teasing you about your cooking, your drawing, your . . ." She wound down, shrugged. "Your everything!" She got up closer, in my face. "You gotta know what's coming next."

I thought of Mrs. Lonigan's puckered-up, steam-cleaned face, her mouth working harder than a snowplow after a blizzard to shovel out all those accusations—"homo," "rubbing *up against her boy*" . . . I felt Lonigan's whiskered jaw as he launched himself at me in the hallway. I shuddered.

"So what? Let them think what they like."

Karen flopped down on the battered old sofa in the corner of her kitchen. "Man oh man, you are something. You wouldn't get the message if it came gift-wrapped in Cellophane."

She was expecting something from me. I could feel it. I just wasn't sure what it was. I put the spoon on the stove, not even caring that it left a sticky, dark splotch.

"I gotta go."

"No, Cisco, listen."

I stopped.

"You ever wonder about me?" she asked.

I shook my head.

"Well, let me be the first to tell you. I'm gay."

Karen glared at me like I was some prize chump. I opened my mouth to speak and couldn't think of a single thing to say that wouldn't sound totally stupid.

"And idiots like Lonigan should be put in their place."

Had someone just put my head on spin cycle? The world was one mixed-up place. And to think I'd come by Karen's to get cheered up.

"Thought never occurred to you, huh?"

I guess there's a limit to what the mind can take in, especially in one twenty-four-hour period. I just wanted to escape.

"Aren't you going to say something?" she asked.

"I gotta go," I said again. "Add some tomato paste to that so it'll thicken up." I dodged her hand and headed for the door. "See you Friday."

"Yeah, sure," she said. "Friday."

Fridays at the Pizza Oven weren't going to be nearly as much fun as before. The entire world had just done an ollie kick-flip and I was having a hell of a time landing it safely.

At home, Delta was tapping away on her computer. The twins were watching *Harriet the Spy*, probably getting all kinds of ideas for ways to torment their friends and neighbours, but I didn't have the energy to care.

"Saved you some dinner," Delta yelled at me as she saw me go by.

She'd obviously decided to let me be. No doubt she picked that up in one of her psychology courses. Give the troubled teenager space. And she didn't know the half of it. I slammed the door to my room and flopped down on my bed. Wondered how life could get so screwed up. First my dad and now my best friend tell me they're gay, like I should have known all along. I mean, what are the odds?

I stared at the ceiling. Wished I were dead. Once again, wished I were anywhere but where I was.

5

Tuesday morning, the twins woke me by bouncing on my chest. "It's snow-ing," they chanted. "Snow-ing, snow-ing, snow-ing. Come on, Cisco, get up!"

This must be what it feels like to be fifty, I thought as I heaved myself into a sitting position and looked out the window. I took a leak, jumped in the shower, forced myself to think about hot coffee and nothing else—especially Rocky. Or Karen. It was a losing battle. Karen's face, wearing a menacing expression, imprinted itself on my brain. When Rocky doggedly shoved her out of the way, my head pounded as if the entire cast of characters were bashing at my skull trying to escape. It was almost a relief when halfway through the shower, someone flushed the downstairs toilet, scalding me.

The twins were already outside by the time I got down for breakfast. Delta gave me a questioning look, then handed me an envelope from the school confirming my suspension.

"Rocky said he'll come by tonight," she said. "He wants to talk to you. What happened to your face?"

"Someone flushed."

"Oh." Her expression turned guilty. Scalded by my own mother.

"Why didn't he show up yesterday?"

"I know this might be hard for you to understand, but Rocky's going through a tough time too."

"Geez. I'm real sorry."

"No excuses, just an explanation."

"Well, you know, maybe I'm looking for some fatherly advice here."

"Sarcasm doesn't suit you, Cisco." She scowled as she read the suspension letter I handed back to her. "I've got volunteer work," she said. "The shut-ins."

She was talking about the two old ladies who lived on the east side of town. She spent two mornings a week picking up groceries and prescriptions, doing light housework and giving therapeutic-touch sessions.

"Girls," she shouted out the back door. "Time for school."

She pecked at my cheek on the way by. "A week will go fast, Cisco, you'll see." Then her Beetle was gone, a puff of exhaust fumes hanging in the air behind her.

Karen and Rocky were on my mind as I tried to concentrate on the January issue of *Gourmet* magazine that Delta had brought home from the library. I tinkered with the idea of submitting one of my original fudge recipes based on two pounds of chocolate, cream and butter. Thought I'd change its name from Triglyceride Surprise to the All My Troubles Lord Will Soon Be Over Fudge. I would do this strictly as a public service. Instead, I passed the morning watching reruns of *I Dream of Jeannie* and *Bewitched*. Then I switched to the Food Network and watched Tyler Florence, Emeril and Nigella Lawson. I love how they make love to the food. I love how they describe the ingredients. Nigella, especially, has a nice turn of phrase. I lost myself in an abundance of colour-ful verbiage. I hung on every word as she described "tender ribbons of rare and rubied steak" or the "glottally thickening wodge of chocolate chips and cocoa" in her chocolate ginger-bread. By the time eleven o'clock rolled around, I had been more or less successful in keeping my mind off of Rocky and Karen. And I was starving.

There was nothing to eat, as usual. At least nothing I wanted to eat. So, I shrugged into my coat and headed to the town square. I'd found some change lying around on the bottom of the junk drawer, counted it up and added some of my own until I'd scraped together eleven dollars. I'd made a shopping list and was looking forward to creating something good, maybe a lemon roast chicken—because as Nigella says, there are few things in life that can't be made better by a chicken roasting in the oven. The snow was pil-ing up and the town looked like the cover of an L.L. Bean catalogue. There really isn't a bad time of year to live in Lovell, scenery–wise. It's the kind of crap that's propping the scenery up that gets to me.

Take the Jewitts, for example. Their house is at the corner, almost on the square itself. They claim they've lived in Lovell for eight generations. Whoop–de–do. Why is it that living in a place forever gives a person a feeling of superiority? I mean, who cares if some mouldy old ancestors cleared the land? What's that got to do with the fact that you beat your wife and smack your kids around?

Merchants were out in front of their stores hoisting shov-els of snow and piling it onto the street for the plows. Mr. Patterson, who runs the pharmacy, was leaning heavily on his shovel, his face florid. He's got to be eighty if he's a day. I was thinking heart–attack thoughts when he purpled up and started to cough.

"Hey, Mr. Patterson," I said as I got closer. "Better sit down."

He cleared his throat and hawked a giant gob into the white snow. "Just a little morning phlegm, s'all, m'boy," he barked at me. "Just clearing out the pipes, just clearing out the pipes." He pulled a cigar out of his pocket and started chawing on the end. He still looked a bit green, though, so I eased his shovel out of his hands and pushed him inside.

"I'll finish up here if you like," I said, pointing to a lady who had piled up a few purchases on his counter beside the ancient bronze cash register. "Looks like you have a customer."

He squinted into the store, rubbing the frosted window like a six-year-old. "So I do." He tottered off inside, calling over his shoulder, "Thanks, Cisco. Take it easy now."

I started shovelling. He hadn't gotten very far, had just scooped a few shovels from the entryway. I got into it, the muscles in my arms working, liking the feel. Despite the cold, I broke into a sweat and in no time I'd cleared about half the sidewalk. Mr. Patterson had lived in Lovell forever, just like the Jewitts. His children had all moved away, and rarely did anyone come to visit him. Lots of the kids were scared of him. He lived in a rundown mansion in "Olde Lovell" and never gave the kids treats for Halloween. I remember him chasing Karen and me away when we were in grade school. The old house had been the scene of countless eggings and other vicious attacks over the years. All because one old guy hadn't wanted to hand out a few suckers. I was thinking of the meaning of all this as I shovelled.

"Hey, girlie man!" yelled someone from the other side of the square.

I kept shovelling, lost in thought about Halloweens gone by, and wondering what Mr. Patterson had gained by being so stingy.

Lonigan, O'Reilly and Lester crossed the square, lobbing snowballs in my direction. One hit me on my swollen nose.

"I said 'girlie man,'" taunted Lester.

I brushed the snow from my nose and eyes. The three of them were coming at me. I dropped the shovel and backed into the entryway of the pharmacy, slipping on the little diamond-shaped tiles. The door opened behind me and the lady customer came out and picked her way across the snowbank toward the hardware store. I grabbed the door and edged inside. Mr. Patterson looked up from his cash register and scowled at me. A snowball hit the window with a tinny splat. Mr. Patterson jumped and peered into the street to see the three of them noisily weaving toward the store.

"Outta my way, Cisco," he said.

I turned from the window and glanced over my shoulder. He was holding a shotgun! My heart stopped. His hands were shaking, his eyes were rheumy and his skin was still the colour of an eggplant. His face looked about as healthy as his judgment. After all, he was about to blast three kids into the next state for throwing snowballs. And, as much as I would have liked him to scare the shit out of these idiots, I really didn't want them dead.

"Mr. Patterson, I'd put that gun down if I were you," I said as I backed toward where he was standing.

"Get out of my way, boy," he answered, raising the gun to his bony shoulder. His face colour deepened, if that was possible.

Lester and O'Reilly were laughing; I could hear the voices getting louder. They had no idea what was waiting for them on the other side of the door.

"Really, Mr. Patterson. You could get in big trouble."

"Quiet down, boy. I got my property to protect."

"You might kill someone here!"

"They come in that door, they take their chances." There was fire in his eyes now.

I was starting to get really worried.

Lonigan rattled the door handle. The old-fashioned bell jingled. Lester and O'Reilly were dancing around in front of the window making obscene gestures. Lester waved a bottle of Jack Daniels—they'd been drinking. Lonigan rattled the door again and yelled, "Boo!"

Mr. Patterson's trigger finger flinched. Lonigan turned the handle. Lester and O'Reilly loomed up behind him. They were coming in. I didn't know what to do. Mr. Patterson started out from behind the counter on shaky legs, his old head wavered from side to side like a turkey's.

The door crashed open. "Stop right there," croaked Mr. Patterson, "or I'll shoot!"

"Geez, Soames," jeered Lonigan, not even paying attention to Mr. Patterson. "First you get two little girls to protect you, then this old geezer. What's up, Grandpa?" He looked at Mr. Patterson. "Playing cops and robbers?"

"It's loaded, Lonigan," I said. "Get out of here."

"Let 'em alone," Mr. Patterson said. "I'll blast 'em to bits."

"Naw, Mr. Patterson," I pleaded. "You don't want to do that."

"Damn punks," he said. "Get out of here."

"Whooooo," O'Reilly said, staggering a little. "I'm scared."

Lonigan picked up a bottle of Pepto-Bismol and threw it at the wall. It splintered, splattering thick, viscous liquid, which ran down the wall in a bright pink river. It looked like someone had stabbed the heart of a giant piece of bubble gum.

I was stuck between an angry and confused old man holding a gun and a trio of drunk punks. Of the two, I guessed old Mr. Patterson was the most dangerous. He was cocking the trigger now.

"Lonigan," I shouted, "duck!"

The gun went off with a loud *crack* and the report knocked Mr. Patterson off balance. Lonigan, O'Reilly and Lester sobered up instantly and started scrabbling for the door.

"Get out of my way," Lester screamed at Lonigan as Lonigan slipped on the Pepto-Bismol and went down, hard, into the pool of pink liquid.

Mr. Patterson had regained his balance and was aiming his gun for another shot. He was like a dog with the taste of gopher guts on its tongue.

"No!" I yelled, and without thinking, threw myself at his ankles.

The gun went off, Mr. Patterson crashed to the floor and the room fell utterly silent. Mr. Patterson lay there, his leg angled off to the side, his eyes shut. It occurred to me that I might have killed him, him being so old and all. Lonigan, Lester and O'Reilly looked up from a heap on the floor. No one spoke.

A hammering on the front window snapped us out of our trances.

"You kids, let us in there!" It was Curt Taylor, the owner of the café.

The sound of a police siren split the air. People were rattling the door, trying to push the jumbled bodies of Lonigan and Lester out of the way. O'Reilly had already crawled to one side and was rubbing his head.

The police arrived at the door, and Lester and Lonigan finally stood up and got out of the way.

"What's going on in here?" demanded Officer Fleming as he pushed his way into the room.

I was on my knees, trying to find a pulse in Mr. Patterson's scrawny old wrist.

"Call for an ambulance, Mike," Officer Fleming yelled outside to his partner. Mike reached for his car radio, its staticky voice chattering impersonally into the frozen air.

"Now, who is going to tell me what happened?" he barked.

"It's all a mistake, sir," I began. Lester, O'Reilly and Lonigan seemed to have lost their ability to talk. "Mr. Patterson thought they were going to rob him."

"And just why was that?"

I started to stammer, wishing one of the others would speak up. I suddenly didn't like the way things were looking. Here I was bending over the unconscious, broken body of a senior citizen, while Lonigan and the others just huddled in the corner looking scared.

The ambulance arrived and took Mr. Patterson away.

Out front, the sidewalks were clogged with people trying to see inside. Lonigan, Lester and O'Reilly were led away and put in separate cars. I was put in the back seat of Officer Fleming's cruiser. Everyone rushed around, a blizzard of officials and busybodies.

I closed my eyes against the flashing lights. I thought of Mr. Patterson's sparrow shins as I rolled into him, of his old-man smell as he landed on top of me.

What if he never woke up?

6

There was no sign of the others when we got to the station. They put me in a small room with just a table and chair. The ceiling was water stained, the cement–block walls completely bare. They called my parents, told me I could have a lawyer if I wanted one. Delta arrived first, then Rocky. Officer Fleming was professional and noncommittal and just kept asking me what happened.

"Tell me again, Cisco, what you did when Mr. Patterson shot at you."

"He didn't shoot at me," I kept explaining, wondering where Lonigan, O'Reilly and Lester were and what they were saying. "He was shooting at the other guys."

"How come you assaulted him?"

"I didn't assault him. I tackled him to stop him from killing Lonigan."

Even though he told me we were being videotaped, it seemed like he wasn't listening. He kept asking me the same questions over and over.

"Right," he said. "Now tell me again what happened when you broke into the store."

"I didn't break in!" I shouted.

Delta gripped my shoulder. Rocky stood beside me, shaking his head, signalling for me to get control. Officer Fleming narrowed his eyes. Suspect shows violent tendencies, I imagined him thinking. It's easy to see how things get out of hand, get twisted.

"You're free to go," Officer Fleming finally said. "For now."

Rocky shot him a look.

You'd never know they all hung out together on weekends, that Officer Fleming was the twins' soccer coach. It was that impersonal.

Lester's, O'Reilly's and Lonigan's parents showed up, yelling, blaming Mr. Patterson, the police and me for everything. By the time I got home I knew one thing. I was in as much trouble as everyone else. Back home, Rocky and Delta went into the den for a summit and I slammed into my room and flopped on the bed.

It was surreal. My parents were downstairs discussing my violent tendencies. Together again. The crazy idea that Karen would be proud of my new desperado image popped into my head. The twins were upstairs, hiding in their room, too afraid to come out and witness the carnage. I wanted to stay hidden forever, but a few minutes later Rocky yelled at me to come downstairs. Rather than cause a scene, I went. Rocky was waiting for me in the living room. I didn't know where Delta was.

"Sit down, son," Rocky said, putting out his hand and trying to pat my back.

I shrugged him off, dropped into the nearest chair and glared at him.

"Look, Cisco," Rocky began. He cleared his throat. "I know this is a difficult time for you."

"You think?"

"There's no need to be a smart-mouth."

I caught a glimpse of red at the top of the stairs. The twins were watching. I drew a breath, bit my tongue, not wanting them to hear how I really felt, and stared Rocky in the eye.

His hair was limp and his eyes bleary. It looked like he'd been drinking, which didn't make sense because Rocky never drank.

"Cisco. I have to say something."

I grunted.

"You've never gotten into trouble before in your life. Now, all of a sudden, you're suspended for a week and under suspicion for attempted robbery and mugging. I'm sorry if what's happening with me is the cause of all this."

"Lonigan, O'Reilly and Lester have had it in for me since grade school," I said.

"I know, I know." Rocky rubbed his stubble, absently, as if surprised to find it there.

Delta came to the door and hovered for a minute, then left when the phone rang.

Rocky turned his attention back to me. "Tell me again what happened."

"Are you serious? What happened at Mr. Patterson's was an accident," I said. "You should know that."

"Look, Cisco, the others are saying you started it all. Mr. Patterson's still unconscious. I know it sounds ridiculous, but right now it's your word against theirs."

Delta reappeared. "That was Brighton," she said. "He'll be right over."

Brighton's the lawyer for the old-age home where Delta also volunteers her time. He's the only lawyer we know.

"This is unbelievable," I said.

Delta sat beside me. She gathered my hand in hers.

I had one of those random thoughts that pop up every so often. This one was about how life is like a masked bandit ready to steal your milk money—just like Lonigan had done every year from kindergarten to fourth grade. On the surface, everything is fine, just hunky-dory. We're all a bunch of cute kids sitting around eating pbj's and eyeing the blocks. Then, without warning, one of the cute kids reaches over and snatches your quarter, or your dessert, or whatever it is you really wanted out of your lunch box, and for the next four years, as far as you're concerned, lunch is hell on earth.

This was a milk-money moment. I mean, the room looked exactly the same as it had two days ago. The corner desk was piled high with papers, file folders, books and magazines. Across the hall, the dining room table was stacked with file boxes and tarnished silver. Dust, as usual, was settled thickly on the tops of the picture frames. Everything and absolutely nothing was the same.

The phone rang again and this time I heard Paris answer it.

"Delta!" shouted Paris. "For you!"

Delta dropped my hand and headed to the hall. "I got it," she yelled up the stairs, and then her murmuring voice ebbed and flowed through the house like wind currents.

"Mr. Patterson's regained consciousness," she said when she came back. "The police are going there now to take his statement."

We resumed waiting. The snow that had caused all the problems had melted as quickly as it had appeared, leaving a dirty grey landscape as the final insult. Finally, Brighton arrived, looking harassed and rumpled. Not a reassuring sight. The next time the phone rang, he took the call.

"Mr. Patterson has confirmed that you weren't one of the boys he thought was going to rob him," Brighton said after he hung up the phone.

"Thank God," Delta said.

"But he did say you were the one who knocked him down."

The old one-two punch.

Delta started to cry. Rocky pulled her toward him and I felt like pummelling someone. I went back to my room and locked my door.

No one bothered me for the rest of the night. I fell asleep around ten, after I finally heard the twins tiptoe past my door.

Wednesday morning. Delta was hunched over some paperwork at her desk when the phone rang, startling both of us into rigid upright postures. We weren't jumpy at all, nosiree.

The twins had already left for school and I had been slumped at the table drinking coffee and contemplating taking up smoking. I saw myself as the star of a French film noir, wrongly convicted of a crime, doomed to a life of trying to clear my name. The skies had turned leaden again and the temperature had dropped, freezing everything in sight. Trees were crystal statues, wires had snapped and fallen. Communication lines were down all over.

I let Delta get it. I wasn't taking calls. I returned to my Paris bistro.

When Delta came back she was walking like she was as old as her shut-ins. Mr. Patterson had slipped into a coma. His children had been sent for. He'd been given last rites.

The Paris dream faded. Harsh reality slapped me square on the jaw. I was in deep shit.

"Brighton said you should lie low for a few days, stay in the house." She stopped. "I can't believe this has happened."

Neither could I.

7

Karen showed up on Thursday around lunch, carrying a giant pizza and six-pack of Coke. I'd never been so glad to see anyone in my life.

"You hungry?" she asked, holding out the pizza like a peace offering.

"Yeah." I smiled. "Come on in."

Never mind that the crust was soggy. Never mind that it was third-rate plastic cheese. Fuhgeddabout the neon-red sauce. It was the best pizza I'd ever eaten.

I was expecting things to be awkward. I was prepared for the worst. But Karen has her own way of doing things and with her second slice she just came out with it.

"You cool with everything?"

I stopped, pizza slice halfway to my mouth. A glob of sauce plopped onto my thigh.

"I think we should talk," she said.

"I guess." I rubbed the sauce off my jeans. "You first."

"I just don't want you to be freaked. Do you get that you're not the only one that this has ever happened to? That Rocky's not the first father to come out? Do you wanna talk about it or anything?"

I had a million questions I wanted to ask. It felt private, all this stuff. I didn't know what to say and yet I wanted to say something.

"You hear about Mr. Patterson?" I asked, changing the subject.

Karen shook her head. So I told her. She didn't flinch.

"He's going to be all right, Cisco. He's the meanest old coot in town. Too mean to die."

I knew she was just trying to make me feel better. I swigged on my Coke, fighting with the lump in my throat. In five days my entire world had been flipped like it was a giant griddle cake.

"I'm glad you're here, Karen."

She smiled.

I sniffed. "About this gay thing," I said, knowing she wanted to talk about it.

"Thing?"

"Sorry."

"I'm just ragging on you, Cisco. Go on."

"You always known?" This was the question I really wanted to ask Rocky.

"Pretty much. But in the last two years? No doubt."

"Your dad know?"

"We've never talked about it. I haven't exactly made a point of telling the world, if that's what you're asking. People talk. Way too much. I only told you 'cause we're tight, you know? And 'cause of your dad."

Kids did talk about Karen. Mostly about how she fought anyone who gave her a hard time. I always admired the hell out of her for never caring what people thought. At least never *seeming* like she cared—which is probably even harder to do, if you think about it.

"That girl could have won the West," Rocky always said, back when she still went to school. The place felt empty after she dropped out. I wanted to be as brave as she was. I wanted to ask her how she did it.

"Look, Cisco. It's no big deal. You're one thing or the other. I'm the other. So's your dad. End of story."

On the other hand, Karen sees things in black and white. I mean, Rocky is my father. He'd married Delta and had had kids. Where did he get off changing his mind? Wasn't it just a little late in the game for that move?

"So what about you?"

I tensed like those guys you see on the bobsled. I mean it. Put me and a board side by side and you wouldn't know which one to hammer into the wall.

"You like girls?" Karen stared me down. Dared me to answer.

"I guess." I shrugged back into the chair, studied the red stain on my knee.

"You guess?"

"I guess." I tried for nonchalant, not wanting to get into it. I took another bite of pizza. It was true—I liked girls all right. I just didn't know what to do with them. They scared me with the way they whispered and giggled and the way they never seemed to go anywhere without a flock of other girls fluffing around them.

"Well, there you are," Karen said. "Nothing to be scared of."

"What do you mean?"

"I mean, Buffalo Bill, that you can go out and wrangle your-self a filly any old time and no one's going to give you a hard time about it. Life's going to be a sail down the river. No upstream slogging for you. You oughta be glad."

"Karen, are you pissed off or something?"

"Just want you to see that you've got it easy. Don't make it hard for the rest of us."

By the "rest of us," I assumed she meant Rocky. And you know, part of me really wanted to get it. I really, *really* wanted to get it.

But I didn't. I didn't get it at all. And that totally killed my appetite.

"Well," Karen said, shoving the pizza box aside, "I'm glad we had this little chat, aren't you?"

"You're a true friend," I said.

She grinned. "Don't take on so much," she said, patting me on the shoulder and batting her eyelashes. "Everything's going to be all right. Another few days and your suspension will be up. You'll go back to school. Mr. Patterson will be back behind his counter at the drugstore getting ready to shortchange his next customer, and you and Rocky will patch things up."

"Gee, Karen," I said, almost buying in, "You sure know how to sweet-talk a guy."

And at that, we both started laughing.

Little did I know, it was going to be a long time before I laughed again.

8

By Friday morning I was even looking forward to work—until Karen phoned and said Pizza Oven would no longer be needing my services.

"But I'm the best pizza maker they've got," I yelled at her.

"Hey, don't shoot the messenger," she retorted.

"Who'd he hire?" I asked. Frank DiMenna never did like me. Thought I had attitude. I heard him telling the dishwasher one night that there was "something off about that kid." I always wondered what that was supposed to mean. Did I smell funny? Like milk with a month-old expiration date?

"No one yet. Listen, Cisco, don't get all het up about this. DiMenna's an idiot."

Sometimes Karen's Wyoming roots bust right out of her carefully constructed punk-rock skin.

"Het up? Geez, Karen, why would I get het up? I mean, I'm suspended from school. Everyone thinks I'm a mugger of helpless old men. I'm guilty until proven innocent. But sure enough, it would be really wrong to get *het up*. Life's one big day at Disneyland right now. As you can see."

"Look, I'm sorry, okay? Let's do something tomorrow. Maybe you can come to my house and watch a movie."

The knot in my stomach shrank just a little. This was a step in the right direction. This was, as Hallmark would say, what friends were for. "Thanks," I said.

"Sure."

Not that I was desperate or anything but as soon as she hung up, I started riffling through my DVD collection. Since O'Reilly worked at the video store on weekends, I sure as heck wasn't going there to rent anything. That left the DVDs I owned. I pulled out *The Godfather*, my first choice. One of my all-time favourite movies. Naw, didn't feel like it. Kept going. *Mr. Deeds Goes to Washington*, the original. I'm a purist, no Adam Sandler remake for me. *Blade Runner*, the director's cut. *The Collected Works of the Naked Chef*. Hold on, I thought. I flipped back to the cover picture of Jimmy Stewart on the front of *Mr. Deeds Goes to Washington*. Made me think of Mr. Patterson and all at once I kind of started feeling sorrier for him than for myself. I mean, poor old Mr. Patterson was pretty bad off. It was the first time I'd really let myself think about it. The more I thought about it, the worse I felt.

I needed to go visit. I needed to tell him that I was sorry, that I hadn't meant to hurt him. I snapped the lid of my DVD case shut.

I would do it. Go to the hospital. Apologize for tackling him. Try to explain. Set the record straight.

You'd think I'd have known better.

First, the hospital's in Burlington and I didn't have any way of getting there. People don't hitch rides the way they used to, back in the sixties when Delta and Rocky were touring around and the whole world seemed ready to buy each other a Coke.

There's a Polaroid around that someone snapped of them thumbing a ride on a highway somewhere out West. There are wildflowers on a hillside in the background, California poppies. Delta told me it was on the way to Berkeley in the summer of '72. So weird to think that there was a time when we weren't worried about terrorists, school shootings, AIDS or anthrax.

Burlington is a forty-mile drive from Lovell and in good weather I could have ridden my bike, but today I was going to have to rely on four wheels to get there. Karen had her licence, maybe she'd give me a lift. I called her back.

"Karen, hey."

"Cisco. S'up?" She barely got the word out, she was yawning so hard.

"What're you doing today?" She didn't go to work until six. "Why?"

"Want to drive me to Burlington?"

"What for?"

"I want to see Old Man Patterson." I thought about telling her that I wanted to say I was sorry about the way things had turned out, but I was suddenly shy about it.

"You think that's a good plan?"

"Maybe not, but I want to go anyway."

I heard her pause, think it over. Karen's like that. She needs to look at all the ways things can go wrong before she makes her decision.

"Sure."

Somehow I took that as a good sign. Like I said, I should have known better.

The roads were slick but not slippery. Karen drove fast, but solid.

"I think you have a future as a trucker," I told her.

"Don't laugh." She shot me a hard look. "Wouldn't be a bad life. I'd like to see something other than Lovell."

"Sorry."

"Don't worry about it."

She geared down. She was driving her dad's old pickup truck. He let her take it whenever she needed it and we drove around a lot, looking for stumps and stuff like that. I keep telling her to sell the sculptures she makes out of dead trees. She says the money doesn't interest her, and that she just wants to remind us that trees are living beings too—and need respect.

Burlington's not a big city, but it's enough bigger than Lovell to make a visit exciting. Under different circumstances, Karen and I would have hit some of the indie music stores, had lunch at a vegan restaurant and checked out the head shops. Today, I was focused on getting to Mr. Patterson. I wasn't a Catholic or anything like that, but I was definitely wanting to see Mr. Patterson and get some sort of absolution. I wasn't sure why, really. I mean, all I'd done was try to save him from getting into a lot of trouble. I had to reconsider my methods, I guess. But still, I hadn't meant for anything bad to happen to him.

Karen swung the truck into the hospital parking lot. "I'll drop you, okay?"

"Aren't you coming in?"

"No, I thought I'd go hang in the doughnut place over there." Karen pointed at a grungy little coffee shop on the corner.

"Please come in." It was hard to ask, but suddenly I wasn't feeling as confident about what I wanted to do. I imagined an even more shrunken Mr. Patterson rising from his bed, pointing his finger and grimacing in ghostly fashion while he told me I had murdered him.

Karen levelled her gaze at me. "Sure," she said.

We sloshed our way through the parking lot, passed the smokers with their wheelchairs and IVs, and entered the lobby, where the sudden hush of serious business enveloped us.

I hate the smell of hospitals. I have ever since I was six and had to have my tonsils removed. The air is dead. It was ridiculous but I felt like crying. The receptionist told us where to find Mr. Patterson.

He was in a ward with what seemed like all the other old people in Vermont. It was not a cheery place—there were tubes and machines and bent straws in plastic cups of melting ice. The nurses' shoes squeaked on the floors and there were get-well cards propped on tables with wheels. I asked where he was, then walked over to the cubicle the nurse pointed at. The bed curtain was drawn around him to give him some semblance of privacy, but in truth, what did it matter? He was in a private world of his own. I had thought he'd be watched full time, but there was no one with him.

Karen had come as far as the door with me, but she decided not to come all the way. She was in the hall, talking to an old lady in a wheelchair. The lady's hair was so thin, you could see pale pink freckles on her scalp. Made me wonder if she'd had freckles as a young girl. I read a book once where some kids asked an old lady to prove to them that she was young once. And no matter what the old lady showed them, they wouldn't believe her. She pulled out ticket stubs from a theatre performance she'd attended sixty years ago. She showed them opera gloves, and toys she'd played with when she was a girl. The kids laughed at her. Finally she hauled out a photograph of herself at twelve, with long ringlets and high button shoes. They said it was some other little girl, that she'd never been young, that she was lying. It made me sad to read that story, just like it made me sad now to look at the lady in the wheelchair with girlish freckles on her scalp. She was about as substantial as a crumpled piece of tissue, sitting there. And looking at Mr. Patterson, breathing shallowly along with the beeping machine, I thought that nobody liked him enough to even care that he might have been young. I studied him until his face went out of focus, and wondered where his kids were. I'd never seen either of them, though the rumour was that he had two sons.

"Hey, Mr. Patterson," I whispered. "I'm really sorry about what happened. I was just trying to stop you from killing someone, you know? I never wanted to hurt you. Boy, I never wanted that. You know, I believe you were young once, Mr. Patterson. I can see how you might have been, all feisty and tough. I bet you were from out west somewhere, just like my friend Karen. Or maybe you came here on a boat from England—I can see how you might have done something like that. I never knew that much about you, and I'm kind of sorry now that I didn't, because it looks like I might never get the chance. But, I'm hoping you do wake up and we can get to know each other." I kind of ran out of things to say at that point. I was thinking about maybe leaving, when the curtains were swished aside and a stout woman stared at me.

"Who are you?" she asked suspiciously.

I was all caught up in Mr. Patterson's life history and I wasn't thinking clearly, because I answered her straight out. "Cisco Soames, ma'am." I don't know why I threw in the ma'am. It must have been the idea that Mr. Patterson might have sailed to America from England, or something.

"Cisco Soames?" Her eyes narrowed.

"Yes."

"The boy who practically killed my father-in-law?"

I stood up and started backing away from the bed. This probably didn't look too good. No, it probably didn't look good at all. In fact, from the expression in the woman's eyes, it was safe to say that things looked pretty darn bad.

"Nurse!" she yelled.

"Nurse!"

I had backed my way out into the hall by this time, but the woman was charging after me, her mouth working, sputtering and damn near foaming.

"Nurse!"

A nurse and two orderlies came squeaking down the hall at double time. Karen, who had been kneeling beside the lady with the pink freckled scalp, jumped to her feet. There was general pandemonium as the stout lady started shouting and calling for her husband, Gerald, to get the hell over here and see if this juvenile delinquent had done further harm to his father.

Another nurse at the desk was on the phone asking for Security, and all the other visitors had shoved their heads out of doors from one end of the corridor to the other. I was struck by how old people and teenagers actually have a lot in common. No one believes them when they say something.

I knew the situation wasn't about to get any better for me. "Run!" I yelled at Karen, and she scooped up her army knapsack and we booted it into the stairwell without even waiting for the elevator.

"What the heck happened?" Karen panted as we spiralled down the stairs.

"Nothing!" I jumped the last three steps and bolted for the lobby.

We careened past the gift shop with the crocheted tea cozies for sale and out into the cold air. The sweat on my skin froze into an icy glaze. We jumped into the truck, pulled out into the street and just made it through a yellow light.

We headed out of the downtown and onto the interstate. No police cars wailed up behind us and no angry, outraged police officers gestured for us to pull over. Our breathing settled down and Karen cranked up the heat to stop me shivering.

"Trouble follows you everywhere, doesn't it," she said. "You checked your horoscope lately?"

Frosted fields whizzed by. I stared out the window and tried to figure out my life. Karen slid into a stony silence. I kept trying to tell her I appreciated her driving me to the hospital, but every time I opened my mouth, no words came out. I was like a fish gasping on a gravel riverbank waiting for the turkey vultures to peck out my eyes.

We rounded the corner into Lovell and Karen started snapping her gum, something she only does when she is really bummed out.

"So, Cisco," she said, the frustration popping with every crack of her wad. "What exactly went on in there?"

"Nothing." I glanced at her, then added, "I swear."

"Something had to have happened or else why would that lady have gone ape-shit?"

"She caught me talking to her father-in-law, that's all."

Karen stuck her arm out and signalled a turn. The electrical in the truck was all screwed up and you never knew which light was going to blink, so mostly Karen just used her arm. We used to joke about sending mixed messages. I didn't think it seemed so funny any more. We pulled up in front of my house.

"You know, Cisco? I'd try to avoid trouble if I were you."

I stared ahead, as if trouble was a bogeyman about to come marching down the street.

"Thanks for the advice."

"Hey." Her voice softened a little. "I know you didn't mean anything by going to visit the old guy, but here's how it had to look. The kid who decked a helpless old senior shows up at his bedside, uninvited. Sort of sneaks in, not telling anyone where he's at. Looks bad, my friend."

"How come you agreed to go?" I counted on Karen and her trouble radar.

"Didn't figure on the crazy daughter-in-law."

"Well, me neither."

She smiled. "Poor Mr. Patterson. He'll probably never wake up. Not with *her* manning the bedside. I mean, would you?"

She leaned across the seat and smacked one on me. I grabbed her hand and we sat there, just staring at the sky. "Gotta go," she said at last. "Can't be late for work."

I watched her drive away. When she stuck her arm out at the corner to signal, she gave me a backward wave. I listened to her truck rattling down the street. Even though I couldn't see it any more, I liked the noise, liked the clouds of exhaust, liked the fumes. Didn't like the empty street that remained behind after she'd driven out of sight.

The house was quiet. For about ten minutes. I barely had time to take off my bush jacket, remove all my chains and start sorting laundry when Delta crashed through the front door. I came out of the laundry room to find her storming down the hall dragging a twin by each hand. She collapsed into a kitchen chair, her face like a slab of marble.

"I give up," she said.

Paris and India stood on one side of the kitchen as if expecting a knife thrower to start lobbing sharp objects in their direction.

"What's wrong?" I asked.

"Shoplifting," Delta said, staring at the twins. "Acting out."

"Huh?"

Paris and India didn't seem as repentant as I would have liked. Smirky smiles jostled for position with their current we're–so–hard–done–by–what's–the–big–deal? expression. I could have told Delta I'd seen this coming, but one look at her told me that this wasn't the time.

"They were picked up in the Inglenook, stealing crystals."

The Inglenook is one of Lovell's very twee gift shops. The only place in town with security cameras and owners so uptight their seams are splitting. This, in spite of the fact that they set themselves up as deeply knowledgeable New Age gurus with a crystal for every spiritual crisis.

"And Mr. Fulton is pressing charges." Delta dropped her head in her hands.

The twins and I stared at each other over her bent head. You can't fool me, I told them with my eyes. You better not even try.

"Where's Dad?" Paris asked. "I want to talk to Dad."

Delta's head came up and she said, "So do I." She waved a hand. "You two go to your room."

Released, the twins shot each other a satisfied glance, clearly under the impression that they were, once again, going to escape with nothing more than a slap on the wrist. They high-fived each other when they thought no one was looking and sauntered toward the hall. I watched them go, figuring I'd have to have one of my brotherly talks with them later. Delta wasn't up to the challenge. It was clear she was already chalking their petty larceny up to a deep-seated spiritual hunger.

Just then I heard little squeaks of alarm and the rattling of their shoes as they clattered up the front stairs.

"Those girls are moving quickly," Delta said absently as she rummaged around in the drawer looking for some green tea. "Maybe they—" She heard a noise outside and stopped.

I followed her gaze out the kitchen window. We looked at each other as a police cruiser came to a stop behind Delta's Beetle. Slowly she reached over and took my hand and we edged toward the kitchen door.

"Well, goodness," Delta said. "What now? I just left the police station. Surely they aren't here over a couple of children stealing crystals."

"Delta," I said, clearing my throat, coughing up the words. "Maybe I'd better tell you a little bit about my day."

9

"You what?" Delta said when I told her about my visit to Burlington.

The policeman banged on the door again. We both stared at it, frozen. Finally Delta broke away and yanked it open.

"Oh, for God's sake, Rick, come on in."

Officer Fleming inched into the back entryway. "I guess you know why I'm here," he said, straining to keep it professional.

Delta raised one eyebrow the way she does when she's bent on conveying just how ironic she considers something to be. "Suppose you tell me," she said.

Officer Fleming glanced my way. "Cisco here is in trouble again."

He said it as if I'd been nothing but trouble my entire life instead of having a bit of bad luck over three days. My friend had a dog once that was the sweetest-natured dog in the world. One day a neighbourhood kid whacked it on the head with a plastic *Tyrannosaurus rex*, then gouged it with a Batmobile and the poor dog, not knowing what to do, snapped at the kid. Nothing serious, just a "don't do that again if you don't mind" sort of snap, and the next thing that poor old dog knew, he was living on some farm in the country, chained to a doghouse, and wondering just what it was he'd done wrong. I could identify.

"He told me about it," Delta said. "He didn't do anything to that old man. He was just trying to see if he was all right."

"Mr. Patterson's son's filed a complaint, Delta. He's asking for a restraining order."

"You've got to be kidding."

"Wish I was."

Officer Fleming told me to stay out of trouble. He tipped his hat at Delta and tramped out to his cruiser. I swear he was measuring me for a collar and leash as he backed away.

"What's happening to this family?" Delta lamented as she flung some tea leaves into an old cracked teapot. She picked up the phone and dialled Rocky. "Damn answering machines," she screamed into the phone, completely losing her cool, unlike anything I'd ever seen before. "Rocky, you need to get over here as soon as you get this message. I mean it." She slammed down the phone and whirled to glare at me.

"Breathe," she commanded.

I breathed.

"Not YOU!" she sputtered.

I massaged her shoulders. She relaxed under my fingers. The kettle whistled and I warmed the pot, dumped the water, added tea leaves and poured more boiling water on top. Delta watched me, her expression considering.

"Come here," she said, after I'd covered the pot with a tea cozy I'd bought at a garage sale. She held out her hand.

I took her hand and sat down.

"I feel so bad about all this," she said. "Are you okay? I mean, really okay?"

There were lots of ways to answer that question. Yes. No. Maybe so. Her way, my way, the right way, the wrong way. I tried figuring it out and couldn't.

So I said nothing and we just sat there. Holding hands.

Rocky came over around seven o'clock. First, he and Delta went into the den and talked to the twins. I sat and surfed through the cooking shows while I waited for my turn. I had just tuned in to Bobby Flay touring around Ireland, when the door opened and Paris and India came out. I checked them carefully for signs of repentance, but wasn't sure there were any.

"Cisco," Delta said.

My turn.

Every time I saw Rocky, my stomach left skid marks on the linoleum. I tried to remember he was my father, even tried to tell myself that he wasn't really living with another man, tried to make believe he would be bunking in with Delta just like before. But, try as I might, you can't not know what you know, as a friend of mine once said. So, with my heart ka-booming around in my chest, I took my seat opposite the parental unit.

"Son," Rocky began, "you're in big trouble."

Delta sat beside me and put her hand on my arm.

"I didn't do anything," I pointed out.

"It's how it looks," Delta said.

"I'm surprised, hearing you of all people say that," I replied. "After all, you're the one who always says we should trust our feelings."

"I know." She wrung her hands, then looked at Rocky, sort of passing the torch.

"What's going on here?" I asked. Something wasn't right. That much was certain.

"We had a talk with Rick and he suggested something that makes sense," Rocky said. His voice sounded dried up.

"Oh yeah? This oughta be good."

Delta rubbed my arm again. "Don't be like that, Cisco. We're trying to find a solution."

"Solution to what? To the fact that everyone in this crappy town has gone crazy?" There was a sick little bubble of puke in the back of my throat. I stared at Rocky.

"How do you feel about going away for the winter term?" Rocky asked.

"Are you nuts?"

"You've heard us talking about Uncle Vincent," Delta began.

"Your crazy brother? The draft dodger? That Uncle Vincent?"

"That's him," Delta said, almost proudly. "You wouldn't actually remember ever meeting him, I guess. You were pretty young the last time you saw him."

"How old was I?"

"Three."

"You think?"

"No need to be sarcastic, son," Rocky chimed in.

I just stared at both of them. Alien life forms must have invaded their bodies sometime during the past week. Neither of them was a person I recognized.

"Anyway," Delta continued, "as you know, Vincent is my older brother. He lives in Canada. On a ranch in British Columbia."

Alien life forms. Definitely. I was failing to see just how this had anything to do with me.

"We thought we'd send you there for the rest of the school year," Rocky said.

Aha!

"So you can get a break from the way things are going

here," Delta said. Tag–teaming their way through the rest of the conversation, they continued.

Rocky: "We called him earlier and he said you could help on the ranch."

Delta: "It's a beautiful place. Up in the mountains, with lots of animals."

Rocky: "You can hike. Go snowboarding."

Delta: "You can go to the local high school. I'm sure there are lots of nice kids up there."

Rocky: "Everyone needs a new perspective sometimes."

Delta: "We just want you to be happy . . ."

Rocky: "You can fly out right after Christmas."

Delta: "We can all visit in the spring . . ."

Rocky: "Chance for a new start . . ."

"NO!" I shouted, discovering my voice lurking just this side of my outrage. "ARE YOU TWO CRAZY? No, pardon me, don't answer that. Of course you're crazy, otherwise you wouldn't think this was such a clever idea. If we're talking positive changes here, how about something a little less drastic? How about Rocky moving back in here where he belongs? How about not taking everyone else's word for what's been happening in my life? How about—now here's something really different—how about listening to ME?"

The two of them stared at me like I'd sprouted Incredible Hulk–like proportions. Not content to stop there, I got to my feet and stomped out. I've always been a reasonable sort of person, or so I thought, but being separated from my family? Well, that was plain vicious! All to go live with some wacko uncle mountain–man I hadn't seen since I was three years old! I crashed into my room and slammed the door. Nope. No way.

Oh, I remember hearing them talk about Uncle Vincent, all right. Uncle Party was more like it. He'd dropped out of the system back in the 1970s, burned his draft card and hightailed it to Canada. Not that I blame him for that. I mean, I wouldn't have wanted to go and fight in Vietnam either. Family folklore being what it is, though, he's become famous over the years for being permanently stoned. Now they were thinking of committing me, Cisco Soames, to the care of this cowboy–pothead?

Nice try, folks, but I don't think so.

10

The plane took off with an exaggerated thrust. Little planes like this were way touchier than the big jumbos. I could practically feel the rivets popping along with my eardrums. At the front of the cabin an ancient flight attendant was demonstrating how to affix an oxygen mask to your face in the event of an emergency. The little yellow cup and bulging eyes made her look Porky Pig-ish. She was nice, though. She handed me some nuts in a little package and a plastic cup with canned orange juice. I clutched the book Delta had handed me in the Montreal airport. I could still smell her musky, incense perfume in the pages. "Here, Cisco," she'd said, passing me the book. "Something to read on the plane." It was *The Power of One*.

I wasn't talking to her by then. I'd toughed out the very unmerry Christmas season, hadn't even tried to go back to school after the suspension ended; instead I'd gotten permission to work at home under Delta's tutelage. I'd even passed my Christmas exams. The fact that Mr. Patterson was still in a coma hadn't added any levity to our home life, but I'd done my best. Just to show everyone how much I valued them, I'd even forced myself to make Delta's vegetarian favourites—chickpea pasta and black-bean stew.

To no avail. In spite of everything I was being shipped to British Columbia. You'd think I would have had some say in the matter, but when it came right down to it, I was still this ridiculous thing called a minor. Somewhere along the way, I stopped fighting it because I figured getting out of town might not be a bad idea. Once I got my head around it, I decided that not having to look at Lonigan, O'Reilly or Lester for six months couldn't be seen as a total negative.

Not that I was letting Delta and Rocky off the hook. If I was going to suffer, so were they. That's just how life works.

The mountains bared jagged fangs below me as the plane winged its way up over the Rockies. I'd insisted they not book a flight before Sunday, even though Delta had pointed out that I wouldn't have any time at all to "acclimatize" before starting in a new school on Monday morning. Like I cared? I was a condemned man, hoping for a last-minute reprieve from the governor. But Delta was in no mood to grant me clemency. Once she decided I'd be better off with this stranger who was my uncle, she wanted no more talk about it.

The flight from Montreal to Vancouver had been uneventful except for some little kid beside me who wouldn't relax. His mother was travelling with him and what looked like a five-year-old who must have been his older brother. The five-year-old dropped right off after a while, but the little guy, whose name was Daniel and who looked to be about two, kept on partying. He had the headphones strapped on and he kept be-bopping up and down in his seat, waving his pudgy little hands as he jived to the beat of music only he could hear. His poor mother looked like she was ready to hand him a Valium or something, but I actually thought he was kind of cute. He had red hair and freckles and made me think of the twins.

I helped the mom off the plane in Vancouver by carrying Daniel who hadn't lost an ounce of energy. They were meeting their dad in the arrivals and I got a squishy lump when I saw them all connected in one big bundle.

The connecting flight from Vancouver to Cranbrook, though?—that was something else. Little planes freak me out, and I swear if I'd reached outside that toy I'd have swiped snow off the mountaintops. I wanted to close my eyes but I was paralyzed with fear. The flight's a short one, only about an hour and a half, so soon we were coming down, zipping between the mountains into the Cranbrook airport.

I waited while they unloaded the luggage from the belly of the plane and saw my duffle bag land on a trolley. I walked across the tarmac into the airport and looked around. Delta had described Uncle Vincent to me, so I scanned the crowd for a tall man with black hair and blue eyes. No one fit that description, though, and I was left standing there while everyone else hustled off into the sunset or whatever it is they do in mountain towns.

I dragged my duffle bag out of the baggage claim area and scanned the airport. Nothing, the place was practically deserted. A light snow started to fall outside the terminal windows and a tinny-sounding recording of "Mac the Knife" drifted out of the snack bar. A guy was in there, hunkered over a steaming cup of coffee, listening to an ancient transistor radio—the kind you see in antique stores. He was fiddling with an antenna and even from where I stood, I could smell the weed emanating from his wool sweater. His hair was shoulder length, completely grey and stood out from his face in spoke-like fashion. He swivelled on his seat and took me in.

"Well, good grief, man, give your Uncle Vinnie a hug!"

The mountain man launched himself off his seat and grabbed me with frightening enthusiasm. He held me at arm's length and laughed. "Sure don't look like a criminal to me. HAR, HAR, HAR, HAR!" His laughter boomed off the ceiling, practically shook the dishes off the counter and stopped everyone within two hundred yards in mid-stride. You could practically hear them thinking, *Criminal, what criminal?*

Uncle Vinnie didn't seem to notice. He hoisted my bag over his shoulder and started for the parking lot, all the while hollering over his shoulder like I was deaf. "Let's get you out to the ranch, my boy. My God, I feel like Father Flanagan in *Boys Town*. HAR, HAR, HAR, HAR!"

I slunk out after him, avoiding the curious stares of airport security as I went by.

His battered truck looked to be about the same vintage as the transistor radio, which he had now propped on the dashboard.

"Get in, get in!" He motioned to me. "Here," he said when I climbed in. "The seat belts don't work, so wrangle yourself to the seat with this." He handed me an old belt.

He turned the truck out onto the street and we buzzed off down the highway. "The ranch is about half an hour out of town," yelled Uncle Vince over the roar of the engine. He kept smiling at me like I was some kind of rare, out-of-season bird.

I stared straight ahead and wondered how hard it would be to hitchhike to Spokane, start a French bakery and make a million dollars. Because I thought if I had to spend even one night under the same roof as this wacko, I might become permanently damaged.

The glistening mountains slid by. At one point I even saw a mountain goat, but didn't say anything because Uncle Vince was too busy singing along with the Rolling Stones about how you can't always get what you want.

"You can say that again," I muttered under my breath.

We rounded a bend and jounced along down a rutted track that was beginning to fill in with snow.

"We'll have to get the sled dogs out soon!" laughed Uncle Vince. He was the type of guy who never spoke in anything but exclamation marks.

A headache was creeping up over my eyebrows, mushing for the frontal lobe.

We came to a split-rail fence and Uncle Vince hopped out and dragged the gate out of the way. "Don't unbuckle your seat belt!" he shouted.

I glanced down at the old belt he'd given me. For the first time I noticed its clasp was a Harley-Davidson with the words *Ride Free or Die* etched onto the metal.

I closed my eyes and tried to think of something positive. Just one thing. But Uncle Vince was back in the car and we were moving forward, bumping along the trail, until we hit a clearing dominated by a large log house that looked like it might have been a lodge of some sort in its day. Thoughts of that movie, *The Shining*, flickered in my brain. The dark was closing in, the snow was getting thicker and there wasn't a light on anywhere, but it was obvious to me that this wasn't ever going to feel much like home sweet home.

"Well, get out!" Uncle Vince yelled.

At the sound of his voice, five huge dogs came howling off the porch, jumping in ecstasy. At least I hoped it was ecstasy. I just hunched down in the car and wished I were dead.

"Come on, come on!" Uncle Vince commanded as he waded off through the snow and the dogs.

I waited until a small glimmer of light appeared through the gloom, then decided that left with a choice between slowly freezing to death and hearing one more blast of Uncle Vince's belly laugh, I'd take my chances with Jack Frost. Bears, I wasn't so sure about, and as I sat alone in the truck, I was positive I could see a dark shape making its way through the pine trees.

I peered through the dark and the snow hoping that I was imagining things, but there was no visibility. Finally I decided I owed it to the twins to at least try to survive, and swatting the snow from my eyes I ran for the cabin. I arrived in the front foyer, breathless and shaking, to be swarmed by dogs.

"And so," Uncle Vincent shouted from somewhere at the back of the cabin, "I got this group of sportsmen coming up this way on the weekend to do some cross-country skiing and a little hunting." He banged some pots and pans.

I headed toward the sound, arriving in the door of what passed for a kitchen, just in time to see him throw something into a bowl and start pounding.

"It oughta be a fine time what with the weather closing in like this. Now, Gorgeous, wait your turn."

I realized he didn't even know I hadn't followed him in from the truck and wondered just how much of the conversation I'd missed. It probably didn't matter, seeing as how he seemed perfectly capable of having a conversation while completely alone, but I was curious.

One of the dogs escaped from the kitchen, a piece of bone clutched between her teeth. This must be Gorgeous. Three other dogs approached when they saw her coming, and she snarled. "Don't look at me," I reassured her when she cast a suspicious glance my way.

I took off my coat, hung it on a hook in the wall along with other threadbare and smelly coats, and settled into a rickety chair beside a round table that was scarred with cuts and actually gouged with initials. Uncle Vincent kept talking and banging and laughing at his own jokes. I thought about hibernating. I seriously doubted Uncle Vincent would even notice if I stayed in bed for the rest of the winter.

"Soup's on!" he announced as he slid a tin bowl of something steaming across the table at me. He then parked himself in the first available chair, and picked up a knife in one hand and a fork in another. All that was missing was the cartoon caption *Let's eat!*

I looked dubiously at the bowl in front of me.

The food was as terrible as it looked. The worst I'd ever eaten. Uncle Vincent shovelled it into his mouth with such speed he probably couldn't taste a thing, and now I knew why. It was rubbery, flavourless and floury, all at the same time, which is a remarkable feat.

"What is this?" I asked.

Uncle Vincent grinned around a mouthful of stale bread. "Great stuff, isn't it? Shot me this fellow back in October and been eating like a king ever since."

"Shot what?"

"Moose! Big guy just over the ridge there. Had me a time bringing him back, but I finally managed it. What? Aren't you hungry?" He pointed at my full bowl. "Never mind." He slid my bowl over to his side of the table. "I can eat enough for the both of us." I watched relieved, as my dinner disappeared down his throat. He finally sat back and patted his stomach. "That's better!" He then scooped up the two bowls, marched over to the sink and tossed them onto a stack that was congealing artistically into a passable replica of the Leaning Tower of Pisa.

"Come on into the other room so's we can get acquainted!" Uncle Vincent shouted as he walked by.

I wondered if he thought I was deaf.

In the front room he was already lobbing logs onto a

blazing fire. "Fine night for a fire! Fine night!" He settled onto the floor, leaned his back up against the old couch, closed his eyes, and in seconds was snoring deeply.

I just stared at him. Now that he wasn't shouting, singing, eating or, God forbid, laughing, I could actually hear my stomach groaning. As quietly as possible, I rose to my feet and tiptoed back to the kitchen. There wasn't much—just a few staples like flour, canned tomatoes, a box of saltines and a bag of oatmeal lurking in the pantry. Even so, it was a vast improvement over months-old moose meat, so I wrestled a pot out of the sink, scoured it within an inch of its aluminum soul and added some water and salt. When the water boiled I tossed in some oatmeal. Scrounging even farther into the depths of the pantry, I discovered some raisins and a few tired-looking almonds, which I toasted over a low heat. There was an apple in the cold storage bin, so I chopped that up and tossed it on top. I laced the whole thing with some maple syrup, and coffee cream that I'd discovered to my surprise and delight in the fridge, then sat down at the kitchen table to eat and take stock.

I was stuck here until June, when school ended. That meant I had six months of this to look forward to. Apart from the sputtering of the fire and the freight-train whistle of my uncle's snores, it was clear the place didn't offer much in the way of entertainment. I spooned some oatmeal into my mouth and wondered what I could do to pass the time other than watch the other dogs watch Gorgeous chew on her bone.

Uncle Vincent was snoring so hard, I just didn't have the heart to wake him, so I picked up my duffle bag and *The Power of One* and set out to find my bedroom.

Upstairs there were six rooms, but only two actually had beds in them, so I figured the one with *Hunters' Digest* magazines and the Bob Marley poster wasn't mine. I tossed my duffle bag into the corner and then, too dispirited to care, crawled into the bed—only to discover that my mattress felt and smelled like it had last been slept in by the moose we ate for dinner.

I closed my eyes and, strangely soothed by the sounds of the honking–whistling–snorting coming from downstairs, I rolled into the trough in the middle of my mattress and fell asleep.

I woke with a feather duster brushing my face and the sound of someone speaking through a megaphone right into my left ear.

"Glad to see you found your room! Now get up and come on down for breakfast. It's time to get you into school. Bet you can't wait for that! HAR, HAR, HAR, HAR!"

I pushed Gorgeous off my chest and opened my eyes just in time to see Uncle Vincent disappearing down the stairs.

In the daylight, the cabin was even more rough–hewn than it had appeared the night before. Other than the kitchen, the downstairs was one big room, with a scarred picnic table at one end, a few sagging armchairs, a threadbare couch in front of a stone fireplace and a smattering of footstools. The windows looked out on an army of pine trees, and a blizzard.

Uncle Vincent had the truck idling when I finally stumbled down the front steps into the snow. The wind howled down from the mountains, bending the tops of the pine trees in half and driving snowflakes the size of dinner plates into the windshield.

"Welcome to January in Canada!" Uncle Vincent bellowed over the sound of ice being scraped from the back of the truck. "Isn't it great?"

The wind sucked up his laugh the way some people say cats suck the breath of babies. Everything was muffled except the whistle of the wind.

"Get in! Get in! Can't have you freezing to death on your

first day on my watch now, can we." Uncle Vincent stomped his feet and shook his shoulders like a gigantic woolly mammoth rising from a millennium's nap. He climbed into the truck, wrenched the wheel toward the memory of the rutted tracks and ground his way along the path, the chains on the wheels slowly gaining purchase. After a quarter of a mile or so, we finally turned onto the highway.

"I'll drive you today, m'boy, but tomorrow you can get the bus! You just have to hike out here to the road and old Christine will stop and pick you up. That Christine, now, is a real nice piece. You'll like her, all the lads do, if you get my meaning! HAR, HAR, HAR." He glanced my way. "Unless you're like the old man, that is. Gotta say, you sure do look like him! My God! You could be Rocky twenty-five years ago!" He reached over and punched me in the arm. "HEY! Don't look like that! Don't care one way or the other, it's all the same to me. You gotta be who you are, and that's a FACT!"

The truck started a slow skid toward a giant rock and I covered my eyes with my hand. Death didn't seem like such a bad thing at the moment—but I didn't want to see it coming. Uncle Vincent wrestled with the wheel and the back end of the truck fishtailed, one tire drifting perilously close to the edge of a giant ditch. Vincent gave the steering wheel another yank, sending the truck into a 360-degree turn. When the truck stopped spinning, we had come to a dead stop facing in the right direction. The wind whistled through the trees. My stomach heaved.

"WHOOOO, boy! That was a little too much like driving in the Daytona 500 for my liking. Give me a horse any day!" Uncle Vincent said, exhaling in a huge *whoooosh*.

We sat there, counting our blessings. Or at least I tried, until Uncle Vincent restarted the engine, dropped it into first and crawled back out onto the road.

I cracked open an eye and looked around. Behind us, the rock wall receded. The outskirts of Cranbrook advanced and Cranbrook District High School came into view. With its square sign and sprawling grey building, the school didn't look much different from Lovell's. Sometime in the fifties a squad of visually challenged architects must have swarmed the continent, throwing up hideous, institutional edifices designed to squelch the creative spirit of generations to come. The Johnny Appleseeds of concrete.

Uncle Vincent's truck skidded to a halt at the front entrance. "Here we are, here we are, the hallowed halls of learning! I'll see you"—he hesitated—"when I see you!"

I guess that meant I was taking the bus home. I watched the truck sputter out of the parking lot and sighed with relief. But when I reported to the office, a middle-aged woman wearing a parka said school was cancelled for the day.

"Snow day," she said, shaking her head.

She came out from behind the desk and held out her hand. "You're the transfer student, right?"

I nodded.

"Cisco, right?"

I nodded again.

"Nice to meet you. I'm Annie Moffat." She pumped my hand. "You're living out at the Treetop Ranch with Vincent Doyle, aren't you? He came by before Christmas and got you registered."

I sighed.

She shook her head sympathetically. "I know, I know." She dropped my hand and patted my arm. "Well, there's nothing going on here today. Tomorrow morning you need to check in with the office or listen to the radio before coming to town. We could have snow days two or three times this week, the way the weather's looking. Some people don't listen when they're told those kind of things." She looked meaningfully out the window toward the parking lot where I'd last seen Uncle Vincent. "But now that I've got you here, let me show you around."

We headed into the hall, which echoed with our miserable footsteps. There was a mural on the wall, which I scanned in vain for any sign of excellent graffiti art. Beyond that, the usual pennants and plaques celebrated sports wins and locked display cases held trophies. We clattered down the hall toward the gym.

"So, Cisco, I hear you're going to be with us until June," said Mrs. Moffat.

"That's right." I wondered how much she knew about me. School secretaries, in my past experience, knew everything. And I mean everything. I glanced her way.

She was bustling down the hall, looking every bit like something out of an episode of *Leave It to Beaver*. I found the thought strangely comforting. Mrs. Moffat made an unexpected left turn. I stopped, backtracked and poked my head into a classroom.

"Cisco, I'd like you to meet my niece, Lara. She joined my family and our school family in November. A transfer student, too. Just like you." Mrs. Moffat beamed goodwill to all concerned.

A waif of a girl with charcoal-coloured hair looked up from a sketch pad. "Hey."

I nodded.

"This is the art room," Mrs. Moffat added unnecessarily.

The PA system crackled to life. "Shit!" swore a disembodied voice. The microphone squealed like it was being given electric-shock treatment. Something crashed and the voice said, "Dammit!"

Lara kept sketching as if this were the typical pattern of morning announcements.

"Annie!" an agitated voice said into the PA system. "Where are you?"

"It's the principal, Mr. Cowan," Lara said without looking up.

"Oh dear," said Mrs. Moffat. "It sounds like he's dropped the PA system again."

"Better go, Aunt Annie."

"Take care of Cisco for me, dear," said Mrs. Moffat, disappearing out the door.

"Sit," said Lara, like she was talking to a dog. "Mr. Cowan's her brother," she explained, nodding at Mrs. Moffat's retreating back. "That makes me the niece of the principal and the school secretary. How scary is that?"

I smiled. She had an eyebrow ring and a tattoo on her wrist that said "Feast." I snuck a surreptitious look at her sketch. It was an abstract drawing of a face.

"That's pretty good," I said.

She grunted. "You draw?"

"Yeah, graffiti."

"No kidding."

"I worked on a mural in my old school."

"So what are you doing here?"

The question I was dreading.

She glanced up from her constantly moving pencil and said, "Don't answer if you don't want to. You don't have to tell anyone anything you don't want to. I didn't when I first got here. So, you want to come over?"

"Over?"

"To my aunt's house. There's nothing going on here. I just came in with my aunt because I wanted to use the art room when no one's around."

"Sounds all right."

"Let's go then." She flipped her sketchbook shut and shoved

the pencil into her pencil case, picked up her backpack and headed for the door. "You don't look like the type who gets all lathered up over riding a few horses and roping some poor old cows. So sooner or later you'll probably get asked what you're doing here by one of this town's Billy the Kid types, and if that happens, I suggest you have a good answer prepared. I'm speaking from experience."

"Aunt Annie," she shouted into the office as we went by, "I'm taking Cisco home with me."

"That's nice, dear." Mrs. Moffat's voice floated out into the hallway.

Outside, Lara flung her hands in the air and hollered into the sky, "Snow forever, you silly clouds." She turned to me and added, "I love snow. It's so peaceful. We don't get snow in California where I come from."

"California?"

She glanced my way. "What? Don't you think I look like a California girl?"

She looked more like a New York street kid. "Uh, no," I said.

She laughed. "Well, at least you're honest."

Chalk one up for me.

"So where are you from?" she asked.

"Vermont."

Her eyes widened. "Another Yank."

"I guess."

"You must be pretty used to snow, then, huh?"

"We have a passing acquaintance." *Passing acquaintance?* In what universe did that line ever pass for cool? I shoved my hands into my pockets, missed Karen like crazy. Some girls are just so easy to talk to.

"So where are you living?" Lara inquired.

What did I have here? A junior Mike Wallace?

She glanced my way when I didn't answer. Raised an eyebrow.

"At this ranch on the outskirts of town," I finally replied, not wanting to appear completely anti-social. "My uncle's place," I added, throwing in a freebie.

"Who's your uncle?" Lara asked.

"Vincent Doyle."

She started to laugh. "You mean you're staying at the Treetop?"

I stopped and looked her over. "Something funny?"

"Sort of," Lara said. "The Treetop is next door to my Uncle George's house. That's Mr. Cowan to you," she added. She paused. "I like you. You seem like an okay guy. Sympatico, even. So I'll give you my story even though you haven't asked. I got kicked out of L.A. because my parents can't stand each other. And now, after twenty years of them not standing each other, they're not going to stand for it any more." She scuffed the snow with her boot. "They're finally getting a divorce. Things got ugly back in the fall, so my mom decided I should come here and stay with her sister." She took a deep breath. "And my dad's coming here for a guilt trip this weekend. It appears he wants to spend some quality time with me. Sort of an apology for booting me out of my own home when he and my mom were about ready to kill each other." She bent down, packed a snowball and drilled a stop sign. "And, I suggested he stay at the Treetop."

I looked at her in surprise. "Have you actually *seen* the Treetop?"

"Yup. Dropped in with Aunt Annie one day. She told me that at one time Vincent used to have lots of guests stay there, that it was a really popular hunting lodge back in the sixties and seventies."

"It doesn't look to me like anyone's stayed there since the sixties," I said. "Your dad hunt much?"

"Never. But it's his latest interest. They come and go—like his girlfriends."

Underfoot, the snow squeaked as if a colony of mice were having an animated conversation. Off in the distance, the mountains glowed in a strange way, as if lit from within, pale golden through the falling snow. The day had taken on a completely surreal quality.

"Don't you think your dad might be a little upset when he sees the place?" I asked, thinking of the dogs, the dog hair and the moose-meat stew.

"Oh, I thought it might be funny to see my dad really roughing it. I warned him that the place was, um, rustic, but he is so bent out of shape about the divorce, he didn't even listen. Now, he's got nine of his friends coming with him. So much for us spending time together. Don't know why I'm surprised. He's always been like this. Like he can't focus on one thing at a time. Especially me."

I didn't want to touch that one, so I shut up. Not my job to get in the middle of a grudge match. I had problems of my own.

We kept walking. Just beyond the downtown, where the older houses gave birth to their younger, newer, plainer progeny, Lara headed up the walk of a giant old brick house and crashed through the door. A boy of around fourteen wandered out from the kitchen.

"Hi, Lara," he said.

"Hi, Greg," Lara said as she shrugged out of her coat. "Meet Cisco. He's a new kid. Just moved here from Vermont. Greg's my cousin," she added.

"Hey," Greg said. He nodded at me. "So how was the art room?" he asked Lara as he headed toward the kitchen. "You guys want hot chocolate?"

"Sure," Lara said.

We trailed after him. Sat down at the kitchen table.

"No hot chocolate mix," said Greg as he opened one cupboard after another.

"Got any cocoa?" I asked without thinking. They both looked at me.

"Uh, yeah," Lara said slowly, pointing at a cupboard in the corner. "In there."

"Well, you can make hot chocolate from scratch," I said, studying my feet and wondering how my tongue would taste when I bit it off.

"No kidding," asked Greg. "How?"

"You mix sugar and cocoa and add milk," I mumbled, calculating how long it would take me to walk the five miles back to the ranch. Barring freezing to death, I might make it by morning.

"We've got lots of milk," Lara said. "C'mon, Cisco, show us how it's done."

"Yeah, Cisco," chimed in Greg. "You've stumbled into the house of packaged foods. If it doesn't come in a box, we don't eat it."

"Naw," I replied. "I shouldn't have said anything."

"Are you backing down?" Greg said, flopping into a chair. "Man, I really wanted some hot chocolate."

They seemed serious. They weren't taking potshots. I began to wonder if they had peppermint extract, marshmallows or whipping cream. Or even some espresso and chocolate for shavings. My head was spinning with visions of thick luscious cups of creamy hot chocolate with a selection of toppings when Lara leaned over and shook my arm.

"You checking out on us, man?"

Greg handed me a can of cocoa. "This the stuff you're looking for?"

I took the cocoa, stood unsteadily and walked toward the stove.

"An artist at work," Lara said in an awed kind of voice. "Stand back. Give him room."

Greg passed me a pot, and I flexed my fingers dramatically, then added five rounded tablespoons of cocoa and some sugar. I was relieved to see the milk was whole and not some thin, blue, low-fat travesty, and made a paste. I gradually stirred in enough milk to make five cups of cocoa. A glance at the open pantry told me that marshmallows fell into the packaged food category. And, wonder of wonders, there were cinnamon sticks. I frothed the hot chocolate with a hand-held egg beater, dropped some marshmallows on top and stirred each cup with a cinnamon stick.

Lara and Greg watched me, speechless.

Lara accepted her cup and took a suspicious sip. Her eyes widened. She took another gulp. Her eyes shut. She reached out blindly for my hand. She reminded me of myself during my Helen Keller days.

"That settles it," she whispered hoarsely. "Cisco, will you marry me?"

Greg laughed. "She always says that when she eats something Mom hasn't cooked. She's proposed marriage to at least ten people this month."

"But this time I mean it," Lara said, taking another sip with her eyes closed.

"Dopamine and serotonin," I said. "Natural feel-good hormones. Come from chocolate."

"So what are you doing here?" Greg asked, obviously enjoying his hot chocolate too.

"Here's your chance, Cisco," Lara said. "Try one out on us."

Greg looked confused. "Try one out?"

"Cisco needs a story. He's not telling why he got shipped here. How about you got arrested for writing graffiti all over the statue of your town fathers?"

"Not bad," I said.

"Or, you could be under arrest for illegal manipulation of chocolate into a habit–forming drug," Greg added.

I didn't actually know what to say. Should I just say, *so, okay, I've been booted out of Vermont because I am a threat to old men?* A riptide of stupid feelings was about to deep–six me. I thought it best to get the hell out.

"Gotta go," I said.

I grabbed my jacket and boots, yanked the door open and stepped onto the porch. I knew an overreaction when I had one, but like I said, I wasn't up for this yet. I could hear Karen's voice. *Just deal, Cisco, okay?* Hoo boy.

Lara came out onto the porch. "Sorry!" she yelled after me.

I gave her one of Karen's backward waves and kept going. Maybe I should open a charm school, I thought. Teach people how to make a great first impression.

I trudged back toward town, having decided to hit the grocery store to add a few basics to the food supplies in Uncle Vincent's pantry. No point in starving while I was here, no matter how depressed I was. I picked up some milk, juice, cereal, bread and eggs, paid with my debit card. Delta had topped up my bank account before I left Lovell, giving me a nice healthy balance for a change. "To be used for an emergency," she had stressed when she told me about it, adding that she was going to let Vincent know I had some "mad money." Well, I was mad, all right. And my uncle's kitchen definitely qualified as an emergency. I stuffed the food in my backpack, carefully arranging the eggs on top. Then, with only a vague idea of how to get back to Treetop, I headed for the highway. Hitching a ride seemed like my only option, so I stuck out a half–hearted thumb, thinking I had as much chance of getting picked up as a T–bone at a vegan buffet.

A battered old pickup skidded to a stop ahead of me. So, like, are the Rocky Mountains the place where old pickups come to die? The truck reversed in a woozy, zigzag pattern and sloshed to a stop inches from my toe.

"It must be Chico!" It was the voice of Mr. Cowan. I'd last heard it belting out of the school's PA system. "Climb on in!"

"Cisco," I said as I opened the door.

"Right, right."

"How'd you know who I was?"

"Annie told me. Said you were tall, skinny and clanked when you walked." He stared pointedly at my chains. "And I've never seen you around before. Only made sense. So, anyway, what are you doing? It's shiver–me–timbers cold out here."

"No buses," I pointed out, stating the obvious.

"Right, right. Well, you could have asked me for a ride. We're neighbours, you know."

"So I understand," I said. "Lara told me," I added when he looked at me questioningly.

"Good kid, Lara. Anytime you need anything, you come on over. In fact, I hear my wife's going to ask you and Vincent over for dinner tomorrow night." Mr. Cowan pulled away from the shoulder in a spray of gravel and slush. "Weather's socking in. It does that in January around here. We may be in for a few days off. I'm sure you're sorry to hear that." He turned and grinned at me.

There's something unsettling about an adult who grins. No one grins, really. Except cartoon characters.

"We've got an A–1 school here, Cisco," Mr. Cowan said, as if I'd asked him to give the old pile of concrete some kind of passing grade. "We aim to keep it that way. We aren't looking for trouble is what I'm saying."

"Neither am I."

"Well, good, glad to hear it." He flicked on the turn signal.

"How's that old fellow doing, anyhow?"

I guess you mean Mr. Patterson that old man I just about killed. I guess you're trying to tell me you've got my number so I better not try anything funny in this A–1 school. I guess you're being real neighbourly and welcoming. Of course, I didn't say any of this. I just grinned back. *Mano a mano.*

"Fine, I guess."

"Unfortunate thing to happen."

"Uh, yeah."

Mr. Cowan looked over at me suspiciously, as if he sensed there was a smartass in his car but he wasn't just sure how to handle it. He steered the old truck right off the road, stopped and put his hand across the back seat.

"Well, I'm glad we had this chance to get to know each other, Cisco." He punched my arm in a jocular manner.

I squinted at him, Clint Eastwood in spaghetti–western number one. Tough as nails. Cigarillo hanging from my lip. Two days of grizzled beard covering my sweat–streaked face.

"So we'll see you later," he added, as if waiting for me to get out of the truck.

"Uh, yeah." I looked around and realized that he'd actually pulled over at Uncle Vincent's driveway. I yanked the handle and the door flew open. I didn't notice the truck was parked on such a steep angle until I toppled backwards out of the passenger seat.

"Watch the first step—" Mr. Cowan bellowed.

Water seeped through my jeans. I'd torn my jacket. Snow settled on my eyelashes. I looked up at the face of Mr. Cowan, grinning down at me from the passenger side.

"—it's a doozie," he chuckled.

I brushed myself off and heaved my backpack over my shoulder, noticing the ooze of broken eggs dripping onto the snow. I slipped even farther down into the ditch.

"See you!" Mr. Cowan said as he pulled the passenger door shut. He gunned the engine, spinning his tires before shooting into the road.

It must be the mountain air, I told myself. Everyone in this place is certifiable. Contemplating just what this was going to mean to my chances of parole made me deeply cranky. The long snowy walk down my uncle's driveway did nothing to improve my mood.

It was peaceful, though, I had to give it that. The wind teased the topmost branches into a soft little dance that sent clumps of snow plummeting to the ground. It looked like the trees were having a snowball fight. Up ahead, smoke snaked out of the cabin's chimney, and I tried to think positively. It would be warm inside. I'd just had a whole day without having to worry about bumping into any one of the baboon brothers. Uncle Vincent was nothing if not entertaining.

I had almost talked myself into feeling glad to be back, when I remembered my uncle's cooking skills. My attitude adjustment, my paradigm-shifting exercise drew to a frosty close when I thought about another dinner of moose-meat stew. So much, as someone once said, depends on dinner. I hoped at least one of my eggs had survived the fall.

The next thing I knew, a lump the size of Milwaukee had taken up residence next to my Adam's apple. It seemed like just too much effort to keep going. I wondered if the twins would miss me if I just sat there till spring. I'd been gone for all of two days and I sure as hell missed them.

The door to the cabin swung open and Uncle Vincent stepped out and scanned the yard. His eyes lit on me and he held up his hand in what I thought was a Black Power salute—him being a child of the sixties and all. But no, it was the phone.

"YO, Cisco," he bellowed. "Good timing! Your mother's on the phone. Get a move on!"

It was amazing how quickly I got to my feet.

It was amazing, I thought, what a little phone call could do.

11

"Delta?"

Uncle Vincent made himself scarce. He started clanging pots, like he was making sure I knew he wasn't listening.

"Hi, Cisco. How's it going?"

"All right."

"How's Uncle Vincent?"

"All right."

Was the entire conversation going to be about nothing? There was a lot of stuff I needed to tell her. Hey, Mom! It sucks here! Or, Mom! The principal's doubling for the town idiot! Or, Mom! We're having moose meat for dinner again. A little pepper steak, seasoned with ptomaine just for fun.

"The girls send their love."

"What are they doing?"

"I bought them a video game."

"You what?" Delta had been death on video games ever since I was a kid. It was a clear indication of just how defeated she must be feeling that she'd bought one for the twins. I could only hope they hadn't talked her into something filled with blood and gore. "Just don't let them spend all their time playing it."

"I won't."

"How's Rocky?"

"He's all right."

I wanted to ask about Mr. Patterson, but I was too scared. I mean, what if he'd died or something? A terrible thought knifed me in the gut. Suppose that's why she'd called? My throat went desert on me.

Three thousand miles away, Delta was silent. I could see her, standing in the kitchen, with only the stove light on. I could see her twisting the phone cord in her hand and scraping at a baked-on spill on the stovetop with her thumbnail.

"There's no change with Mr. Patterson," she finally said.

I clenched the phone a little tighter.

"They don't know if he'll regain consciousness or not, Cisco."

I stared into the black night.

Behind me, the pots in the kitchen suddenly ceased their clanging. Time and space buckled under me and I sank into the chair.

"I never thought it would come to this," I said.

Sniff. "Me either."

Expensive silence.

"Well, how's school?"

"Not bad." Sometimes, the only acceptable answer is a lie. And that's the truth.

"You like it there?"

"Great, what I've seen of it. Snow day."

"Oh."

"How're you, Delta?"

"Oh, fine. You know how it is, January blahs."

"Tell me about it."

"Are you sure you're all right?"

"Look, I better go. Sounds like Uncle Vincent might need some help in the kitchen." Massive understatement.

"Cisco, I miss you."

"Yeah. Me too."

After I hung up, I wandered back to the kitchen, but Uncle Vincent was out in the yard, splitting kindling.

"Want to help?" he shouted from behind a stack of logs.

I could just see his axe rising and falling. Up and down. Up and down. Like he was conducting some sort of woodland orchestra.

"Sure," I said. As I approached the pile, Uncle Vincent's head appeared.

"Great! I could use some extra muscle around here. Like I told you, I got a party of ten sportsmen arriving for some skiing and hunting this weekend. Maybe you can come along one afternoon. Carry some gear."

I shook my head. The thought of shooting anything creeped me out. But I could see this was Uncle Vincent's way of making me feel a part of things. I turned my shake into a nod.

Uncle Vincent kind of squinted through the swirling snow, assessing. "Great!" he said and handed me the axe. "You get chopping and I'll get dinner." He trudged off into the gloom.

I stared after him, my mouth open. Talk about Murphy's Law. Me the wood chopper and him the cook. Just another sign of how the universe was seriously out of whack. *Whack!* I swung the axe and sent a sliver of wood rocketing into the trees. *Whack!* The next blow missed completely.

Whack! Hit that sucker dead centre and split the wood in two clean pieces. I stared at the axe in surprise. Had to admit it felt good. I wondered whether if Mr. Patterson died or something and I had to live here forever I'd get used to moose meat and lumpy beds.

Probably, I decided. The thought scared me half to death.

12

Turns out, Mr. Cowan was right. When I woke up and turned on Vincent's radio, the local station was announcing that Tuesday was another snow day. Uncle Vincent, curiously enough, was nowhere to be found.

With nothing else to do, I was sitting hunched over *The Power of One*—poor Peekay was getting his head bashed in again by the kids at boarding school. I didn't think I'd be finishing this book anytime soon. I mean, really, it wasn't the happiest book to be reading for a kid in my predicament. I was wondering how else to spend my day in the sensory deprivation chamber that was my Uncle Vincent's cabin during a blizzard, when someone barged in through the front door.

A giant stood there, a Bigfoot ice-sculpture. The guy had to be six foot seven, with a head the size of a hot–air balloon. "Who're you?" he asked, shaking his coat so that ice chips flew everywhere.

"Who're you?" I retorted.

"Name's Virgil," he said, holding out his paw. "Live in a cabin up the mountain a ways. Got a little stir-crazy with all this snow and thought I'd hike down to see how old Vincent's doing? So, like I said, who're you?"

"I'm Cisco," I answered. "I don't know where Uncle Vincent is. I haven't seen him yet this morning."

"*Uncle* Vincent, eh? Well, well, well. Nice to meetcha, there, Cisco." He took off his coat and hung it on the back of a chair he pulled over to the fireplace. He pulled a hunk of ice off his sleeve and chucked it into the flames, where it sizzled like a hotcake on a griddle. "Didn't know old Vincent had any relatives in this part of the world."

"I'm from Vermont."

"Vermont, you say?" Virgil turned and looked at me, hands on hips. "So what are you doing here?"

"Just staying here for a few months."

The man dragged the entire couch toward the heat and sat down. He yanked his boots off and waggled his toes in front of the fire. "Pull up a seat there, Cisco." He motioned to a spot beside him.

I stayed where I was, looked over my shoulder for Uncle Vincent. Just where the hell was he, anyway?

The man studied me for a minute, then shrugged and said, "Suit yourself. So where'd you say Vincent was?"

"Don't know." Fact was, I *didn't* know. He hadn't been in the house when I'd gotten out of bed that morning. I hadn't lived there long enough to know whether or not that was unusual. Knowing what I did of Uncle Vincent, however, it didn't strike me as something anyone needed to worry about.

"Come from the States myself," Virgil said.

"That's nice," I said.

"Yep. Me and your uncle came up here back in the sixties. Man, those were the days. Escaping the crazies who wanted us to get involved in a war that was nobody's business."

He paused. His eyes had a faraway look and were misted over. "Your uncle and I met on the road. We been helping each other out ever since."

A door slammed in the back of the house. "Cisco!" shouted Uncle Vincent. "Day's half over. You better be out of that bed!"

I glanced at my watch. It was 8 a.m. Uncle Vincent called from the kitchen. "You out there?"

"Yeah," I yelled back.

"Good thing it's a snow day," Vincent yelled again. "How do I know that?!" he bellowed rhetorically over the sound of barking dogs. "Well, I'll tell you. I'm a fast learner. I checked it out on the radio before I left you to your beauty sleep. I've been up for hours! Already got us a fish!"

"Ice fishing," Virgil said knowingly.

Uncle Vincent appeared in the door. "Hey, Virge! Meet the nephew here?"

Virge leaned over and smacked me on the back. "Sure did. We been having a great little chat. Say, boy, did I tell you I come from Louisiana?"

I shook my head.

"I fry up a mean mess of catfish, given half a chance. I can do the same with whatever your uncle's caught there."

I looked at Virgil with new respect. A man who knew food.

"I bet old Vinnie here's been trying to serve you up that godawful moose stew he passes off as edible."

I nodded. I couldn't speak—I was that choked up.

"Well, how's about you an' me seeing what we can do with the morning's catch? That's assuming our boy Vinnie actually has some food in the place for a change."

"Sure!" I hoped I didn't sound too eager, gave thanks that I'd thought to stop at the grocery store the day before. Four eggs had survived Mr. Cowan's neighbourly ride home.

Virgil pushed himself to his feet. I followed him into the kitchen.

"I was training to be a chef back in Louisiana just about the time they drafted me," Virgil said as he slit the trout's belly. "I was in no mood to be sent to some country I'd never even heard of." He opened the fridge, snooped in the pantry. "Hey!" he yelled at Uncle Vincent. "You stock up for the kid?"

Uncle Vincent parked himself on the counter. "Naw. Kid thought he'd starve eating my stew. He bought his own food. How do you like that?"

"I like it," Virgil said. "You got style, kid."

He dipped the trout in some milk, then some cracker crumbs, and sprinkled it liberally with salt and pepper. Already my saliva glands were kicking into high gear. The butter sizzled in the pan. I watched in mute admiration as he lobbed the fish into the hot butter and threw together the fixings for hot biscuits.

We sat down to the first real meal I'd had since I arrived. Uncle Vincent even managed a decent pot of coffee to go with it.

"So, Virgil," Uncle Vincent said after we'd finished, as he picked at his teeth with a fish bone. "You all set for this weekend?"

"Sure am," Virgil said.

I leaned back, my stomach nicely full. "This weekend?" I asked, feigning ignorance.

"Yeah," Uncle Vincent said, squinting at me. "Remember I told you about this party of hunters I got coming up from the States? Gotta thank old Cowan's niece Lara for that one. She's been staying here for a few months, while her parents sort themselves out. She's from la-la land. You'll probably meet her, Cisco—she goes to your school. Tiny little thing with big eyes."

"Met her yesterday," I said.

"Nice job," Uncle Vincent said. He nodded approvingly and

swatted me on the back. "Kid's a fast mover." He winked at Virgil. "One day and he already hooks up with the coolest chick in town. So what'd you think, Cisco my man?" He didn't wait for an answer before plowing on. "Anyway, her dad was coming up to see her and she suggested he stay here. Pretty damn sweet of her, if you ask me."

"Sweet," I repeated. I wondered if I should tell him that, as far as I could tell, sweetness hadn't entered into it.

"Said her dad had promised to come visit her at the beginning of the year. She wondered if I'd ever thought about taking in guests." Vincent took a swig of coffee. "Told her that's exactly what I used to do, until every yuppie from here to Vancouver decided they wanted 'amenities' and started booking into all these phoney ranches that have sprung up around here." He paused, shook his head in disbelief, then continued. "Designer water, Italian sheets and hot tubs, for God's sake!" He rolled his eyes skyward. "Anyway, Lara said her dad wouldn't want any of that and she got right on the phone and called him. Set it all up." He beamed.

Like a lamb to the slaughter, I thought. This definitely had grudge match written all over it.

"So, Virgil," Uncle Vincent said, slapping his hand on the table. "What do we need?"

Virgil handed Uncle Vincent a list. I watched, fascinated, as these two shaggy-looking beasts talked over the merits of organic versus nonorganic flour.

"Whatcha' gapin' at, boy?" Virgil growled at me, interrupting my thoughts.

"Nothing." I closed my mouth and started clearing the table. "I'll wash."

Virgil harrumphed behind me. "Ain'tcha never seen a man cook before?"

Truth was, I hadn't really, other than on TV. Oh, sure, I'd

seen the pizza guys slap the dough around. But as for food that really tasted good? Nope.

"Well, I'm going to get going," Virgil said. "I got a leak in the roof I've got to fix before the weather really gets bad."

I choked on my last swig of coffee. Before the weather really gets bad? How much worse could it get?

Virgil strapped on his snowshoes for his trek back up the mountain. Just as he was leaving, he slung his giant arm across Uncle Vincent's shoulder and said in a hushed voice, "Don't worry, man. It's all going to be fine. You'll see."

Uncle Vincent squinted into the thickly falling snow and shrugged. "Well, I guess it's got to be," he muttered.

Now, just what did he mean by that?

Uncle Vincent gave Virgil a last wave, then turned to me. "Hey, Cisco!" he shouted, his mood undimmed. "Now, how's about a little music?"

He grabbed his guitar and flopped down in front of the fire. By the time he'd reached the 99th chorus of "100 Bottles of Beer on the Wall," I wondered if I should tell him about my misgivings. But what would I say? Maybe things would work out all right. Maybe Lara's dad wouldn't mind an "authentic" ranching experience. Maybe he'd surprise us all, including Lara. How well did she even know her dad? How well did I know anyone, come to think of it? I mean, people are full of surprises, and I know what I'm talking about. Maybe, maybe, maybe . . . But no matter how hard I tried to convince myself otherwise, I seriously doubted a happy ending was in the cards. I was just about to say something when the phone rang. It was Mr. Cowan, and true to his word, he was inviting us over for dinner.

"Sure, sure, George." Uncle Vincent's voice attacked the phone like it was breaking and entering. "See you later!" He crashed the phone back into its receiver and turned to me.

"Got a summons from your principal." He laughed. "Hey! Don't worry. Old Bessie's a fair cook. Plus they got kids. One's even about your age. And George said Annie and Lara are going to be there. Won't be a total waste of time, eh, Cisco?"

Vincent pushed off from the windowsill he'd been leaning on and strode over to a closet to pull out a pair of skates. "Here! George said we'd be doing some skating before dinner."

He tossed me the skates. I stared at them in horror. I hate skating. Never did like it, from the time I was a kid. It meant hockey to me, and if there's one thing in this world I really hate, it's hockey. Or maybe it's hockey players. I know, I know. What kind of fifteen-year-old boy doesn't like hockey? Believe me, it's a question I ask myself regularly. The point is, though, I don't skate. Not very well, anyway.

I headed upstairs, hoping to avoid further discussion of sports of any kind. Lying down, I attempted to banish the image of Lonigan's cheerful face as he body-checked me into the boards in midget hockey or his sneak attacks with his stick. Oh, such pleasant memories.

Around four, Uncle Vincent hauled me out of an enjoyable sleep. I was dreaming of home, and Rocky and Delta were telling me that this whole thing had been a giant mistake. Delta was setting the table and the smells coming out of the kitchen were complex, yet inviting. The twins were playing Jacks on the kitchen floor and Rocky was strumming away on the battered old guitar that he brought out for special occasions. I was carving a little soap statue. Who knows why I was carving a soap statue. I just was. It was a perfect family scene—right out of *Arthur* or something. I dug down deeper, wanting to keep it from dissipating. I reached for a disappearing fragment, the fading strain of a song, the softness of India's hair . . . against my leg?

"GORGEOUS! Get off your cousin!" yelled Uncle Vincent.

I opened an eye. Gorgeous was dug in against my side, her tail thumping steadily. Uncle Vincent loomed in the doorway.

"Cisco," he continued, "time to get going. Can't sleep your life away, son! Didn't anyone ever tell you that's a sign of depression?"

Holy Holden, I thought. Will this nightmare ever end?

"See you downstairs!" Uncle Vincent turned and clumped down the hall. Gorgeous hesitated for a moment. But only a moment. Then she was off the bed and scrabbling down the hall as fast as her four feet could carry her.

I flopped back and stared at the ceiling. If only, I thought. If only . . . If only *what*?

All the if only's in the world weren't going to change a damn thing. Rocky was still going to be over in Stowe eating fondue and drinking mulled wine, for God's sake. Delta was still going to be racing around looking after everyone else but her own goddamn family. The twins were just going to have to find their own way through it. And me? Well, I was about to go get looked over by the whacked-out principal of Nowhereville High School. That's the trouble with dreams, Mr. Freud. They show you just how far reality is from what you really want out of life.

"Cisco! You got lead in your ass? Get a move on!"

I stuffed my feet into three pairs of socks, grabbed my parka and headed for the stairs. Uncle Vincent was already outside, surrounded by dogs and peering into the sky.

"Snow's letting up," he reported.

"Great," I said.

He handed me a pair of snowshoes. "Here! Strap these on! We'll be going overland."

I had always thought snowshoes were more of a decoration thing. I mean, the only time I'd ever really seen a pair was when they were hanging in the pseudo lodges that catered to the New Yorkers that Vermont is full of.

Snowshoeing was about what I expected. It was like walking with fishing nets strapped to your feet. Uncle Vincent carried on a conversation by yelling over his shoulder. Every word got swept away by the wind and I had no idea what he was saying. I struggled along through the powdery snow with one eye on the mountainside. I mean, avalanches, Uncle Vincent. Ever heard of those? Every once in a while one of his great booming laughs reached my ears and I'd glance up, fully expecting a thundering mass of snow to pulverize us. The dogs ran along beside us, excited to be on this crazy walk. As was Uncle Vincent.

After forty-five minutes of serious exercise, we arrived at a house set back from the road. It looked way more normal than Uncle Vincent's pioneer cabin. It had curtains in the windows, a driveway and a garage and everything. Mr. Cowan was standing in the window watching for us. The minute he saw us, he opened the door and shouted to go around back. There were other people skating down at the rink. Several adults, including Mrs. Moffat and a few kids my age.

Uncle Vincent was already lacing up his skates by the time I half slid down the slope toward the skaters.

"Working up an appetite, my boy?" he yelled as I got closer.

A girl skated over to the edge of the ice and grabbed onto me as if she was going to fall. "Hi," she said.

I took her to be Mr. Cowan's daughter, because she had the same face. I mean it. They were identical.

"I'm Leslie."

"Hi," I said.

"This is Lara," she said, pointing at another girl who was wobbling toward us. "She's my cousin from L.A. Doesn't skate too well."

"We've met," I said, nodding at Lara.

"Come on!" Leslie whooped and skated away.

Lara gave me a sympathetic look. "My mom, Aunt Annie and Uncle George grew up in this very house," she said. "My mom's the only one who got away!"

"On the lam from the education police," I said.

Lara smiled. "Some fun." She held out her hand. "Shall we?"

I grabbed her like I was a drowning man and we started off slowly together. Greg skated by, pushing a hockey stick, took one look at my ankles touching the ice, nodded disgustedly and skated away. Lara squeezed my hand encouragingly.

"He's a good guy but hockey is his life. No kidding. His life!"

Uncle Vincent sailed toward us, then deked away at the last possible second. Funny, har, har. Leslie swooped in from behind, grabbed my right hand and tried to tow Lara and me along.

So, of course, I crashed. Backwards, onto the ice, in about as stupid a fashion as possible. I stared at the sky while the whole world circled around and around and around. . . .

Lara knelt beside me, prodded my arm.

"You okay?" she asked.

I mumbled something about comets colliding.

Uncle Vincent's face appeared over me. "Well! Looks like your skating's over for today!"

He reached down and hauled me to my feet. Mrs. Cowan clucked over me and kept talking about concussions. Uncle Vincent waved away her concern.

"Nonsense!" he shouted. "Kid's fine!"

For once I appreciated his lack of concern. I wished everyone and everything would just go away and leave me alone.

13

"Some fun!" Uncle Vincent said as he parked himself beside me.

I could hear Mrs. Moffat and Lara laughing out in the kitchen. Mrs. Cowan was chopping vegetables for a salad and Mr. Cowan and Greg were slapping the hell out of a ping-pong ball in the adjoining sunroom.

I moved the ice pack from the back of my head and tried to decide whether he was delusional or just plain nuts.

Leslie came in with a bowl of hot buttered popcorn and flopped down in front of the fireplace. She offered it to me. Uncle Vincent made himself scarce, something I was beginning to see he was very good at. I crunched on the popcorn and tried to think of something—preferably witty—to say. Leslie rolled over on her stomach and poked the fire. A shower of sparks rose up the chimney. She had extremely blonde hair and bright blue eyes. Her eyebrows were very arched, making her look like she was just about to ask a question. I kept fighting the impulse to say, *What?*

Finally Leslie said, "Lara's stuck here. Her parents are getting a divorce. They wanted her out of the way while they work things out." She peered into the kitchen as if checking on Lara's whereabouts. She lowered her voice and added, "I think her mom's cracked up and her dad never even came to visit her for Christmas. Lara was extremely disgusted with that move."

"Oh," I said. Some girls are like that, I've discovered. Ready to give each other up and not even think twice. I'd have to make sure the twins knew better. Lara came in from the kitchen and sat down beside me. Up close she smelled nice. Like cinnamon. I noticed Leslie watching us, sizing the situation up and not liking what she saw.

"So, Cisco," she said, "how do you like living with your uncle?"

"It's all right."

"Just all right? You mean you aren't loving it?" The sarcasm coated every word.

"Not loving it, no," I said, trying for a noncommittal type of honesty. The minute I said it, though, I felt kind of bad. Uncle Vincent was trying. I guess I had to give him that. Would it have killed me to say I was having the time of my life? Which wasn't a total lie, in a negative sort of way.

"Yeah. He is a little odd." Leslie raised her eyebrows a fraction of an inch higher, then rolled over on her back and propped herself on her elbows. "My dad says he's got lots of worries right now. You should be nice to him."

"What kind of worries?" There was no shortage of moose meat as far as I could tell.

"Oh, you know. The usual."

Hmm. The usual. Well, let me see. That could be your father's just come out of the closet. Or, no. How about this one? You're sent away because the town police take the word of a couple of drugged-up bullies over yours. And, oh! You put a helpless old man into a coma and he might even die.

"Sure," I grunted.

"Money, I guess," Leslie continued. She sat up, crossed her legs, leaned forward and whispered. "I overheard my mom and dad talking last week. Seems like he's behind on his taxes or something. He runs this ranch, right? Only no one's been coming to stay for a long time. Until Lara talked her father into coming up next weekend. That ought to be good." She glanced at Lara, then continued. "Dad said it's because your uncle's sorta weird, you know?"

"Shh!" Lara said.

We all turned and looked at the door. Uncle Vincent was standing there. I didn't much like the expression in his eyes. In particular, I didn't much like the way he was looking at me.

"Hi!" Leslie said brightly. "Want some popcorn?"

"Dinner's ready," Uncle Vincent said. He kept watching me.

I dropped my eyes. I knew when he was gone because the light from the other room hit me square in the face.

"Ugh!" groaned Leslie as she sank down on her back. "Creepy!"

"Do you think he heard?" whispered Lara.

"He heard," I said.

"Who cares?" Leslie demanded. "We only said the truth."

I couldn't help but notice that now that the shit was about to hit the fan she was using the royal "we."

"I'm starving," Leslie said and headed for the door. "Come on, Lara."

Lara glanced at me, then got up and followed her cousin to the kitchen.

I stared after them, thinking. So Uncle Vincent had money worries. That meant I might get sent home sooner than I'd thought. Well, sorry, Uncle Vincent, but that suits me just fine.

I stood up and brushed off my pants. After all, I wasn't the one gossiping about my uncle's money troubles. I was just being a good listener.

I joined everyone else in the kitchen. So that's what Virgil meant, I thought, when he said everything's going to be all right. Lara's dad and his friends must be paying big bucks for a hunting vacation in the Canadian Rockies. It was all starting to make sense. So maybe, I decided, I shouldn't say anything to Uncle Vincent about Lara not being totally forthright with her dad. Let what will be, be.

I mulled this over while I loaded up my plate with chili, salad and cornbread. It wasn't until I was on my second helping that I noticed something.

Uncle Vincent was nowhere to be found.

"He went home, Cisco," said Mrs. Cowan when I asked. "Said he felt a little tired."

I put my plate down. Lara stared at me from across the table.

"I'll run you back after supper," volunteered Mr. Cowan. "You can't snowshoe through those woods after dark and in this storm."

Sure enough, it was snowing again. Harder and thicker and blacker than ever. I'd seen lots of storms in my time. After all, I come from Vermont, where winter was practically invented. But never anything like the endless, thick cloud of flakes that blew in from some sort of overtime snow factory on the top of this mountain. It seemed hopeless.

It all seemed hopeless.

"Thanks," I said. I noticed Leslie was picking at her food the way all girls do. And suddenly I was really, really homesick for Karen and her putrid cooking.

At least with Karen you knew where you stood. And that seemed really important right about now. There was none of that game playing that goes on with the Leslie type of girl. I hadn't thought Lara was that type, but I was beginning to wonder.

The evening wound down quickly. Vincent's departure had put a freeze on all the nonstop fun I'd been having. As soon as dinner was over, I asked Mr. Cowan if he'd mind taking me back.

"Probably a good idea, with the storm and all," he said cheerfully.

It was like some kind of freaky *déjà vu* when Mr. Cowan dropped me at the top of the road to Vincent's cabin. I checked warily for unexpected ditches before getting out.

"The truck can't make it through there tonight, Cisco. But just follow the fence and you'll get there. Wear the snowshoes."

I strapped the snowshoes on in the headlights of the old pickup, waved goodbye, then started down the road. It was the second time in two days that I'd hiked down this road in a blinding snowstorm. The first time, I was cold, lonely and miserable and dying to get to the cabin. This time, you could add embarrassed to the list.

I tried to remember what else Delta had told me about her brother. Older than her by five years. A loner. Once gone from the States, he'd never been back. Still, Delta had been to visit him a few times. I had gotten the impression she was totally fond of him.

I guess Uncle Vincent had already gone up to bed, because all the lights except the one over the front porch were turned off. I slunk up the stairs so quietly I didn't even rouse Gorgeous. Then I lay in my bed and watched the snow until I fell asleep.

14

"Let's get something straight," Uncle Vincent said the next morning as he poured himself a cup of the brown water he passed off as coffee. He'd been waiting for me when I came down for breakfast. For once he was talking in a low voice, a deeply unsettling experience.

"I don't need anyone talking about my money problems."

I wondered if I should point out that I had just been listening. But from the look on his face, I guessed not.

"Sorry," I mumbled.

He nodded. "Radio says it's another snow day. I'm going out for a little while. Don't burn the place down."

Har, har, I thought as I watched him climb into his truck and plow his way through the deep snow out onto the highway. I picked up my uncle's guitar and began strumming away. While I strummed I considered a few things.

One: I was stuck in some kind of *Little House on the Prairie* time warp. There was no TV and therefore no VCR, no DVD player and no video games. It goes without saying that there was no computer, but I'm saying it anyway. There wasn't even a radio, except for this piece of memorabilia from the last century that probably belonged in the Smithsonian. There wasn't a cell phone and there wasn't even a record player.

Two: It was deathly quiet. Especially without Uncle Vincent around.

Three: There were hardly any people here.

Four: I might starve to death on my uncle's cooking.

I wondered where he had gone and how long he was going to be away. Then, I wondered what I was going to do to fill my time. A few jigsaw puzzles were lying around, but to be perfectly honest, I've never liked puzzles. Colossal waste of time. Why spend hours sticking all these teeny tiny pieces of cardboard together—pieces that are diabolically designed to look almost identical—only to shove it all back into a box? I passed on the puzzles. Started writing a letter to Delta, but gave up. I knew I really wasn't ready to deal with that yet.

Around noon, with the snow still falling and boredom creeping up on me, I decided I'd go for a walk, maybe figure out where on the mountain Virgil lived. See what he might have cooking. Literally.

I suited up, taking a positive attitude toward mastering the snowshoes. The dogs milled around, sensing an opportunity to get outside and chase a few snowflakes, so I let them come with me. I felt almost jolly as I crossed the front yard and headed for the path into the woods that I'd seen Virgil take the day before.

I hiked for over an hour. All uphill. I was sweating like I'd just come out of a sauna. Somewhere at the last turn, even the dogs gave up and turned back toward the cabin. Wind howled through the trees and I remembered that the one time I went camping with the Boy Scouts, the leader, nerdy

Mr. Mitchell, kept yammering on and on about hypothermia. Being a smartass ten-year-old, I'd listened not at all. Snatches of that yammering were coming back to me now—especially words like *death* and *wind chill* and *dampness on skin*.

Turn back, the sensible part of my brain commanded.

One more turn, came the override from command central, a.k.a. stubborn, stupid and self-destructive teenage thought impulses.

So on I went.

Had the temperature dropped? My teeth started to chatter. The forest thickened. A wind with a bite like a tyrannosaurus clamped down on my head.

Lines from a Robert Frost poem we'd been forced to learn in fifth grade circled round and round in my brain. Woods filling up with snow and miles and miles of knee-deep powder to slog through before sleeping. Something like that.

I like poetry. Another unbelievably uncool thing about me. Just add it to the list. Again I considered turning back, but the thought of the empty house and Uncle Vincent's disapproval sent shivers down my spine. I turned and looked behind me. My footsteps were just about filled in. Would I be able to find my way back?

I stopped and listened. The forest was deathly quiet. The tree branches blocked whatever light was left behind the thick snow and clouds. The forest primeval. Another poet said that. I heard what sounded like barking and thought maybe Gorgeous had come looking for me. I held my breath, listened to the sighing of the trees and strained to hear another bark. At first, all I could pick out of the wind was the sound of creaking branches and the occasional *swoosh* of snow falling in a sheet from the pine needles. But then, in a momentary lull, I picked up the sound again. It was a dog, barking frantically. Insistently. A series of high-pitched dog yelps.

I pushed my legs through the snow. It was as if I were dragging two freezers behind me. When I stumbled out of the forest, a border collie ran around me, not even bothering to sniff at me. It ran a few paces ahead, then doubled back. Again and again. I kept losing sight of it, the snow was falling so hard and fast, but it always returned for me, cocking its head the way dogs do when they're trying like mad to convey a message. *Follow me!* was the message I was getting.

"Okay, okay," I muttered under my breath. "I'm coming!"

As if someone had upended a snow globe then turned it right side up, the snow suddenly settled around me and I could see that dead ahead was a tiny log cabin, no bigger than a one-car garage.

The dog started growling and yipping at my heels as if herding me. I tried to ignore her, which made her even more aggressive. She leapt at my sleeve and grabbed it with her teeth.

"Hey now!" I yelled, trying to shake her off.

She started backing up, the cloth of my jacket clenched between her jaws.

"Let go!" I shrieked.

I was so busy trying to shake her loose that I didn't even notice the man until I brushed his leg with my snowshoe and toppled over him, the dog still fastened to my sleeve.

"Virgil!" I yelled.

He was out cold. His forehead was streaked with blood and he was almost covered with snow. Beside him was a ladder.

The dog whined. *Over to you, Human,* it seemed to say. *Do something.*

I dropped beside Virgil and felt for a pulse. Mr. Patterson's fragile old wrist zipped into my mind. I shoved it away. Virgil's pulse thumped reassuringly under my fingers.

Well, at least he was alive. Now I had only one problem.

Well, one *urgent* problem, that is. I was going to have to move this mountain of a man into the warmth of the cabin before he froze to death.

"Virgil," I yelled, knowing it would do no good whatsoever.

Virgil, Virgil, Virgil, the mountains whispered back.

"Wake up," I croaked, kneeling back down and staring at the sky, just as it started to snow. Again.

15

There was no time to waste. Virgil was practically frozen. There was no guessing how long he'd been lying there.

I ran to the cabin and pushed through the door, hoping to find a phone. The cabin was bare, electronically speaking, leaving me with no option but to find a way to drag Virgil in out of the cold. I needed a toboggan or a sled or something.

Frantically, I headed for a shed that hugged the treeline. The door was blocked by snow and I fell to all fours, then dug as hard as I could. By the time I finally had cleared enough snow to open the door about a foot, sweat was dripping down my back. Inside the shed, it was dark and the floor smelled like mouse droppings and wet earth. Blindly, I felt my way around the wooden walls, hoping I wouldn't trip and fall and crack my head open on a saw blade or an axe. Crazy ideas chased each other around my brain. Virgil and me found dead in the spring, our badly decomposed bodies savaged by marauding animals. I could just see them trying to figure it out. A murder–suicide? Who killed whom? And why?

My toe jammed up against a wall and I groped to see if anything was hanging on it. A toboggan! I let out a whoop and the dog appeared, whining urgently at the door. I squeezed out of the shed and plunged through the snow, sinking to my knees with each step.

I finally reached Virgil and positioned the toboggan beside him. I pushed and pushed, trying to roll him onto it. I couldn't budge him. Leverage! I remembered my fifth grade science project on pulleys, gears and levers. I ran to the cabin and grabbed a rain barrel from the kitchen. There was an axe by the fireplace, and I brought it outside and hacked the ladder into two long pieces. I stuck one end of the ladder under Virgil and used the barrel to provide the leverage I needed. He lifted slightly. I tried again, using all the strength I had left. He rolled onto his side and I pushed as hard as I could. He completed the half-turn and lay face down on the toboggan. I dragged him to the cabin, then heaved the toboggan over the threshold and out of the snow. I threw a couple of logs on the glowing embers in the fireplace. They immediately sparked to life.

I rushed around the cabin looking for blankets, grabbed everything I could find, and made a bed on the floor in front of the fire. I cut Virgil's frozen coat off his body, then tipped him off the toboggan onto the makeshift bed. His feet were red. Better than blue—that much I remembered. I tried to recall what to do to bring back circulation. Warm water, I thought. Did he even have plumbing? What if he never regained consciousness? What if he'd snapped his neck and my moving him had paralyzed him for life? What if he had frostbite? What did you do about that?

I suddenly wished I'd been a better Boy Scout.

Virgil moaned.

At first I thought I was imagining things, but the dog's ears were pricked forward and she was in that half–crouch that border collies are famous for.

"Virgil?" I said, leaning forward.

He opened his eyes and put his hand up to his forehead. I'm not an expert on head injuries or anything, but I think that's a pretty good sign.

"Are you all right?"

"Do I look all right?" Virgil demanded, closing his eyes again. He opened them and stared at me. "How in the devil did you get here?"

"I was out for a walk."

"Out for a walk." Virgil moaned. "I think I broke my arm." He nodded at his left arm. The dog nudged Virgil's good hand.

"It's okay, Hazel," he said in a low voice. "The last thing I remember, I was trying to fix a hole in the roof."

That explained the ladder. "Well, it looks like you fell. You knocked yourself out pretty bad. I don't know how long you'd been lying there."

"You carried me?"

"Toboggan," I said, pointing. It lay in a melting puddle of snow at the front door.

"Smart thinking, for a Yank." Virgil nodded. "You better splint up this here arm."

"Uh, sure. Just how do I do that?"

"Get a couple of sticks from the wood over there. Cut 'em so they're flat. Then rip up a sheet and bind the arm. Don't worry. Take your time. I'm not going anywhere."

I cut the sleeve of his shirt and practically passed out at the sight. A bone was sticking out of the skin, just above the wrist.

"Worse'n I thought," muttered Virgil.

"Geez" was all I could say.

"I think we'd better get help," Virgil said.

"I don't suppose you have a cell phone?" I asked.

Virgil shook his head.

"High-speed access?"

Virgil closed his eyes. I guess it wasn't the time for humour.

"That means I'll have to hike back down the mountain. Find Uncle Vincent."

"Better wait till morning," Virgil said.

One look at the bone glistening in the firelight told me just how much it had cost him to say that.

"Can't have you getting lost on the mountain."

He had a point there.

"Give me a shot of whisky," he said. "There's a bottle in the cupboard."

I crossed the kitchen and found the bottle, brought it to him. He drank and lay back.

"We're in a real situation, here, Cisco. This arm isn't good. I can't move it. You're going to have to pull me down the mountain on that toboggan. I can tell you which way to go, but I'm warning you, we've got a rough day ahead of us tomorrow. Breaks like this one—" he nodded at his arm—"can get infected." His voice was fading.

I started thinking about shock and hypothermia and limbs getting amputated.

"Plus, my ankle's sprained."

I looked down. His right ankle was the size of a melon.

"This is a hell of a situation you've gotten us into, Ollie," I said.

He tried to smile but it turned into a wince. "Quoting Laurel and Hardy at a time like this. You're one hell of a strange kid, you know that?"

"I'm old before my time," I told him.

"Get some rest," he mumbled. "We're leaving at first light."

Sure. Rest.

I sat in the chair all night and listened to his breathing, watching for signs of shock. What I wouldn't have given for an Internet hookup. I watched each twitch and grunt like the dog, who never closed an eye. What did I know about shock? I was fifteen and the only thing I associated with the word was Howard Stern. I watched the sun rise and as soon as it looked like there was enough light to see my way down the mountain, I knelt beside Virgil.

"Virgil?" I whispered. His skin was clammy and his breathing shallow and rapid. "Virgil?" I said again. *Wake up!* I wanted to scream at him. *Tell me what to do!* He opened an eye. "Think you can make it?"

He shook his head. "You better go without me. But do me a favour and don't get lost. Take Hazel with you. She knows the way."

"Need anything before I go?"

"Water."

I filled the bucket with snow and left it to melt.

"You might want to reconsider a phone or something," I said.

"Cisco, please."

"I'll be right back," I said, trying to smile.

"I'm counting on it. Hazel, go!" he said to the dog. She was on her feet, watching, head cocked, trying to understand. "Go with Cisco. Find Vincent!"

She nuzzled his hand and licked his fingers. He scratched between her ears and said again, softly, "Go find Vincent."

With one last look at Virgil, the dog was out of the cabin and on the trail. I didn't have time say goodbye.

I was putting on snowshoes. Then frantically trying to catch up.

She was a brown and white streak, but she knew I was important so she kept doubling back to urge me onward.

Now and then the dog went in a direction I wouldn't have chosen. My heart kaboomed around inside my chest cavity like it was a hundred years old and had never done a second of exercise in its life. Which wasn't, sadly, far from the truth.

It felt like forever, but I think it was only a couple of hours later when I broke free of the final treeline and saw Uncle Vincent's cabin ahead. A police car was parked in the driveway and people were milling around, carrying snow-shoes and revving snowmobile engines. The looks on their faces when they saw me were, to put it mildly, a study in contradictions. *Holy shit, the kid's okay! Now let's kill him!* That sort of thing.

Uncle Vincent was walking toward me, his face grimmer than the damn clouds. Before he opened his mouth, he saw the dog. She was pretty hard to miss, actually, since she was barking and twirling around in this chasing-her-tail kind of circle that meant *something's really wrong here.*

Vincent grabbed my shoulder and said, "What's happened?"

"Virgil's hurt," I managed to gasp out. "He fell off the roof. I found him yesterday and stayed with him last night, but I couldn't get him down the mountain. He sent me for help."

After that, I collapsed, but not before the dog looked at me in disgust and resumed her barking, circling dance. I think I passed out then. I'm not proud to say it, but I was done in. It was out of my hands now and the whole world just kind of disappeared for a while.

When I woke up, I was on the couch in front of the fire. Mrs. Cowan was sitting on the footstool. She was knitting. I felt I'd stepped right into a parallel universe and that if I looked hard enough I'd see a comb and a brush and a bowl full of mush. Just like in that storybook Delta always read to the twins called *Goodnight Moon.*

"Hi, Cisco," she said when she saw my eyes were open.

"Hey," I said, trying to sit up.

"Feel better?"

Other than my muscles had seized up, making movement impossible, I was fine. "How's Virgil?" I asked.

She shook her head. "They brought him down a couple of hours ago and took him to the hospital. Your uncle's there with him. I don't know any more than that."

"Is he going to be okay?"

"I hope so."

I lay back and closed my eyes. Why couldn't people lie? Why couldn't she just say he was going to be peachy?

"Your mother called while you were sleeping. I said you'd call when you woke up." She reached over and smoothed my hair, just like she was related to me or something. "Do you want to call now?"

"In a minute." I was too tired to get up. I shut my eyes and it seemed, suddenly, like everything that had happened to me in the past month was taking a curtain call.

There was Rocky, pacing around and telling us he was moving out. That he was gay. My eyes began to sting, and my gut seized up.

There was Lonigan, his forearm jamming my windpipe, hissing into my ear that I was a homo.

And there was Mr. Patterson, looking pasty grey and yellow at the same time. Skinny and rickety like a tree eaten from the inside out by termites! Welcome to the cast! *I only wanted to help*, I said. *You helped fine, Bonehead*, he jeered, jabbing his shaking finger with the long yellow nails that old men seemed to acquire. *You helped just fine.*

Delta. Yes, you! How could you cook up this crazy idea of banishing me to this mountaintop with Mr. Personality?

The more I thought about it, the only one in this production who was at all normal was Gorgeous.

Mrs. Cowan was patting my shoulder and making sympathetic noises. "Tsk, tsk. There, there. Hush, hush."

That's right, I thought.

Hush, hush.

And a bowl full of mush.

16

"Virgil's going to be all right."

I heard Uncle Vincent talking to Mrs. Cowan as she put her coat on. I glanced at the clock. He'd been at the hospital the whole day. It was after five.

"Thank God Cisco happened to hike up the mountain yesterday," she said. "I don't like to think about what might have happened if he hadn't."

Uncle Vincent grunted something in response. I couldn't hear what it was, even though I was practically cupping my hand against the wall. For a man with a ten-decibel voice he sure could talk quietly when he wanted to.

The door closed. Then he was in the living room, rubbing his hand over his unshaven cheek. He bent over and poked at the fire, then turned to study me.

"Well," he said, "how's it feel to be a hero?"

"Sore."

He laughed, then reached over and clasped my shoulder. "You saved Virgil's life, Cisco. That's pretty amazing karma."

"Is he okay?" I asked.

"Going to be fine, thanks to you. Doc expects a full recovery," he paused, poked the fire again, then said, "Mrs. Cowan told me you called Delta when you woke up. You have a good talk?"

"Yeah." Had I. I could still hear Delta's sobbing on the other end of the line.

"I wonder if there's some kind of checklist," Uncle Vincent said reflectively, "where if you do a good thing it cancels out something bad you might have done along the line."

"Interesting idea." I thought about Mr. Patterson.

"Well," Uncle Vincent said, slapping his knees. "Enough of THAT! Want some food?"

"How about I cook?"

Uncle Vincent looked at me. "You cook?"

I detected a tone that went beyond simple curiosity and verged on disbelief.

I guessed I might as well come clean. I had no interest in starving. A near brush with death will do that to you.

"Yeah," I said.

"I mean," Uncle Vincent said, "REALLY cook?"

"What do you mean *really*?"

"Like, good food. Things you might get in a restaurant?"

"Yeah, I guess."

He leaned back and closed his eyes. "Cisco," he said quietly.

"Yes?" I whispered, looking around. Was he about to tell me some deep, dark family secret?

"I never knew you cooked."

"I never knew you cared."

He opened his eyes. "YOU," he said, making me jump, "just might be the ANSWER!"

"And the question was . . ."

"HOW THE HELL AM I GOING TO OFFER GOURMET MEALS TO MY HUNTING PARTY, WITH VIRGIL IN THE HOSPITAL?"

My ears were ringing. But I had one thing straight. He wanted me to cook for strangers. Not just for me and him. Uh-oh. No way.

I must have been shaking my head, because his smile faded.

"What?" he asked. "You won't do it?"

"It's not that I won't," I said. "I'm not sure I can."

"What do you mean?"

"I've never cooked for anyone but the family."

"What do you mean?"

"I got burned a few times."

"Burned!" He started to look worried. "The food?"

"No. Never mind."

"What are you talking about?"

I'm talking about third grade when Lonigan found out I'd made the cupcakes for the Halloween party. I lived with the name Cupcake for five years after that. Then, when I started working at the Pizza Oven, they'd given over to Dough Boy. Oh, and don't forget the time Lonigan, O'Reilly and Lester sneaked by the house when everyone was out and found me baking cookies. . . . No, let's not get into that.

"Look, Cisco, I need your help here. It's hard to ask, man, but I'm in a spot. As you heard the other night, I'm behind in some payments, and on Saturday, Lara's dad and a group of his friends are coming up from California. They're expecting certain, um, amenities. Like good food."

"How good?"

"Um, five-star."

"*Five-star?*"

"Well, I lied a little."

"A little?" I thought of the moose–meat stew.

"Well, Virgil's a damn fine cook, as you saw."

"Yeah, but do you even know what five–star means?"

"Awww, who cares? We just want to give 'em food that sounds fancy. I'll keep them out hunting and hiking all day. They'll be too tired to tell five–star from two–star. You'd just have to put some decent grub on the table."

He didn't get it. He truly didn't get it. Whatever Lara had said, these people were probably expecting a real Rocky Mountain High. As I now understood, any hope of Vincent actually salvaging this weekend had lain in Virgil's hands. And all they were going to get was me. I shook my head.

"No way, Uncle Vincent. It's not going to work."

"Cisco," he said. He was on his feet now. "You've got to help me out here." He slapped my shoulder and strode off into the kitchen. "There's a reason for everything, my boy! And that's a *fact!*"

I shrank down into the cushions.

I have a vivid imagination that plays a lot of very nasty tricks on me, almost as if it were an evil twin. Right now it was having an enjoyable time conjuring up the hundreds of ways I could humiliate, torture and otherwise destroy myself by trying to convince anyone I was more than a hobby cook. Burned rack of lamb, shrivelled vegetables, unleavened bread, flat soufflés. The list was endless.

Uncle Vincent was thumping around in the kitchen.

"*I feel good!*" he sang. "*Now let's knock on wood!*" He poked his head out the door. "Things are looking up, thanks to you, my little godfather–of–soul–FOOD!" he cackled, then disappeared.

Life is a cosmic joke, Rocky likes to say. And most days, I decided, the joke was on me.

"So," Uncle Vincent said, coming back from the kitchen, "what exactly can you cook?"

He'd calmed down some and was taking a saner approach. I had to be grateful for that.

"Look, Uncle Vincent," I said. I'd decided to take the direct approach. "I only cook for fun. I'm not a pro."

"Fun!" Uncle Vincent nodded encouragingly. "That's exactly what I'm looking for. Fun!"

"Other than tossing dough around at the Pizza Oven, I don't have any experience cooking for groups."

"Doesn't matter." He scratched his stubble. "Look, I don't want to force you into this or anything . . . but–" He sighed. "It's hard for me to tell you this, Cisco, but if I don't pull this off, I'm going to lose it all." He waved his hand toward the window. "I've lived here since '68. I've always gotten by, but these last few years have been lean. Thanks to Lara, I finally got this booking and it means big money. Almost eighteen thousand dollars."

"Eighteen thousand?" I forced myself not to look around the cabin.

"Hey! I'm offering a real wilderness experience here."

"I'll say." I thought of the dogs and the plumbing.

"No need for sarcasm."

"Sorry."

"Well then. Part of the package these guys are expecting is gourmet dining in the wilderness. It looks like that's up to you!"

I put my head in my hands. Maybe ostriches have the right idea. Only, I've heard they don't really do that–someone made it all up. After all, even a bird's got to know that troubles just don't disappear because you can't see them.

"Let's sleep on it!" Vincent said.

I sensed him standing up. I felt him leave the room.

I didn't know just how it had happened, but suddenly I was in charge of saving my uncle's life.

I'd already saved Virgil's, I pointed out to whoever was up there.

There's only so much one teenager can do.

17

Friday morning dawned clear and cold. I hadn't slept for one second, I'd been so busy thinking about food.

"Let's make a list," I said when Vincent stumbled into the kitchen. When in doubt, make a list. A motto to live by.

"List," Uncle Vincent echoed, scratching his head. "That's GOOD!" He ripped open a paper bag, got a pencil out of the drawer and handed it to me.

"How many people are coming?"

"Ten."

"When are they arriving?"

"Tomorrow morning."

 I gulped. My hand shook.

"Hold on, hold on." Uncle Vincent patted the air with both hands. "Don't lose it now."

"Do you have any idea what's involved in cooking meals for ten people?" I stopped. *I* didn't even know what was involved.

"We'll get some help," Uncle Vincent said when he saw my face.

"Like who?"

"What about Lara?"

"Lara?"

"After all, it was her idea! Maybe she can move in for the week. Really get reacquainted with her dad. Do some dishes." He rubbed his hands together in a maniacal fashion. "I knew I liked that girl!"

"Do you think Lara was completely frank with her father about what this place is like?" I asked, trying to inject a moment of sanity into the madness.

"Well, probably. She did tell him not to expect the Taj Mahal."

"What exactly did she tell him?" Hel–lo, Uncle Vincent? Reality check.

"What exactly are you getting your shorts in a knot for?" Vincent demanded. "Who knows what she said? Who cares? They're coming, that's all that matters."

Maybe Vincent was right. Maybe that was all that mattered.

"Where are you going to put everyone?" I asked, giving up and entering into the world of the permanently delusional.

"There're five extra bedrooms upstairs," Vincent pointed out. "Once you bunk in with me, that is."

"What about beds?" I asked, choosing not to dwell on that eventuality and thinking these guys just might be expecting something other than the floor to sleep on.

"I got connections," Vincent answered.

I was beginning to wonder if Uncle Vincent was chairman of the local chapter of the mafia.

"Like what?"

"Got a friend who's a liquidator. Got a line on some mattresses. They're arriving today." He looked at me as if the only barrier to success was my unaccountable stubbornness.

"I don't know—"

"We've got to TRY!" yelled Uncle Vincent.

"All RIGHT!" I yelled back. "Do you have any, uh, cook-books?"

He looked at me as if I'd asked for books on embroidery.

"Never mind," I muttered. "Go away and let me think."

"Sure thing," he said. Then, whistling for the dogs, he headed out the back door.

I watched him go, then stared at the brown paper bag that was gutted and filleted on the table in front of me. I picked up the pencil and wrote, *HELP*, then scratched it off with a hundred violent strokes. I thought for a minute, then wrote, *veal chops with Roquefort*. Not much can go wrong with that. It was a start. I felt better already.

Next, I wrote, *chicken with forty cloves of garlic*. Easy peasy, as Jamie Oliver would say, and ingredients even the Cranbrook grocery store would have on hand.

By the time Uncle Vincent stormed back into the kitchen, I'd planned a week's worth of menus. So they weren't gourmet, but where was I going to find radicchio or truffles or even salmon in the mountains in January?

"Well, let's get shopping," he said, folding the list and putting it in his pocket.

"That's going to cost a lot of money," I pointed out.

"Well, we'll cross that mountain when we get there!" Uncle Vincent said evasively.

The plows had cleared the roads and there was a fair amount of traffic coming and going. "What about school?" I asked as we passed the high school. The buses were lined up getting ready to take kids home. "Looks like the snow days may be over." In all the excitement I hadn't even thought about school. Now I was truant as well as delinquent.

"School can wait," Uncle Vincent said as he skidded to a stop in front of the grocery store. "Stay here. I got to make a few arrangements."

I was shivering in the truck, amusing myself by drawing graffiti in the mist my breath made on the window, when a face appeared in front of me. I jumped, bumping my head on the rearview mirror.

"Hey there," Lara said. She yanked open the door and climbed in. "Move over. Heard about Virgil. Glad he's okay. How does it feel to be a hero?"

For some reason an image of Mr. Patterson popped into my head. He was wearing the baggy blue smock he had on when I visited him in the hospital. His bandy legs were hairless, like those hairless dogs you see in magazines. On the other hand, his eyebrows stood at outraged attention. He had a gash on his bald spot, like he'd hit it on a cupboard door. Hey! I thought. Where the hell did you come from?

"I wouldn't exactly call me a hero," I said, thinking Mr. Patterson might totally agree with that statement. I shifted uncomfortably. Lara watched me, her eyes penetrating my brain. I wondered if she was making her acquaintance with Mr. Patterson, who seemed to be about to take up permanent residence in my head. I'd heard about stuff like this. Paranormal stuff. It would be just my luck to get hooked up on some sort of metaphysical channel with a comatose senior citizen. If this had to happen, why couldn't I have at least connected with Kurt Cobain? Or even better, Julia Child?

"How come you weren't in school today?" Lara asked.

I didn't want to tell her Vincent had other plans for me at the moment, so I just said, "Slept in."

"Well, you didn't miss much. Everyone's wondering about this new kid who rescued Virgil. Virgil's kind of a legend around here, living alone on the mountain the way he does. Now you're a legend too." She stopped talking and studied me carefully. "So, I guess you get to meet all the kids on Monday."

I couldn't tell her just how much I was not looking forward to that, so I just sat there.

"So are you all ready for my dad?"

"Yeah." I shoved Mr. Patterson into the corner of my head, told him to take a hike, find some other kid to bug. Tossed him the idea of paying Lonigan a little visit. Then I focused in on Lara. "Are you?"

"I guess."

Didn't sound like it to me. I shut up, not having much talent for small talk.

"You want to come over to Aunt Annie's? Maybe create a chocolate martini?" Lara asked.

"Ha, ha. Thanks, but I'm waiting for my uncle. We've got some shopping to do."

"Yeah?"

"Groceries," I said, leaving it at that.

"Groceries," Lara repeated, looking at me like she'd just put two and two together. Or maybe the equation went more like this: Vincent minus Virgil equals Cisco. "Ohhhh . . ."

Uncle Vincent arrived at the window. "Okay, Cisco, we're all set. Well, hel–LO there," he said, winking at Lara.

"See ya," Lara said, backing out of the car. "I better get going."

"Something I said?" Uncle Vincent asked after she had left. He thought for a minute. "Did you tell her you're going to do the cooking?"

"She figured it out all by herself," I said. "Like it was HARD," I yelled at him when he gave me an evil stare. I jumped out of the truck and headed for the store.

Uncle Vincent followed me with the list.

As we piled the stuff in the cart, I prayed I wouldn't forget anything. When we arrived at the checkout, I held my breath. This wasn't going to be cheap.

"Six hundred forty–two dollars and thirty–one cents," chirped the cashier.

Uncle Vincent turned white. He held up a finger, winked at the cashier and said, "Just give me a moment with my nephew here." He pulled me over away from the checkout.

"Pay her," he said.

I looked at him like he'd lost his mind, which clearly he had.

"Can you pay her?" he repeated.

Then I got it. He was expecting me to pay for this from the money Delta had given me when I was banished.

"Cisco," he said, nodding at the cashier who was waiting expectantly, "we're family. I need you to do this for me."

I couldn't have turned any redder than the tomato I was gripping in my hand. I glanced down and thought ugly thoughts about Uncle Vincent.

Then I pulled out my debit card and handed it to the cashier.

"This is my nephew," Uncle Vincent suddenly decided to announce to the entire store. "He's a great chef!"

The cashier giggled, and behind her the bag boy cringed with embarrassment on my behalf.

I kept my head down and headed for the door.

Uncle Vincent could carry out the damn groceries all by himself.

He looked kind of sheepish when he finally got in behind the wheel. Neither of us spoke as we drove out of town and headed back toward the mountain. We even unloaded the groceries in silence. The evening dragged on, and on, and I was totally prepared to remain speechless for the rest of my life, but Vincent finally spoke.

"Listen, Cisco. I'm sorry."

I sighed.

"I'll pay you back as soon as we get the money for the week. I'm picking everyone up at 10 a.m. tomorrow. We'll, uh . . ." He hesitated, then pressed on. "Need lunch."

Ker-thump answered my pounding heart.

"I'm going to bed," I said.

"Get your sleep, kid." Uncle Vincent nodded like he'd suggested it. "You're going to need it."

Later I lay thinking in bed. The worst that could happen was that I might fail, big time. Visions of soggy bread danced through my head. Best-case scenario was, I might even enjoy it. There's nothing to it, I assured myself. I fell asleep reviewing my menus—and woke at dawn, panic stricken.

How was I going to pull this off?

Uncle Vincent was already drinking coffee. If he'd slept last night it didn't show.

Before he left for the airport he grabbed my hand. "See you later, partner!" Then he thumped down the steps. Minutes later he gunned the engine and was gone.

Leaving me and my anxiety totally alone.

I started by making homemade bread. While it was rising, I diced, chopped and sautéed vegetables for *soup au pistou*, which is really just a fancy vegetable soup—a little something I'd picked up from one of Jacques Pepin's cookbooks. I got the stock simmering and whipped up a batch of my favourite toll-house cookies. By the time I finished, I had flour from one side of my face to the other. I'd been taking a lot of rather deep frustrations out on the bread dough.

At noon, everything was ready. The bread was still warm, the soup was simmering and the cookies were lined up on the cooling racks. I was pacing the floor like an expectant father.

Through the window I saw Uncle Vincent arriving in a minivan. Where had that come from? Then, remembering how he'd called in a few favours, I supposed he'd strong-armed some poor schmuck in town to lend it to him. It's amazing how you can pull a semi-credible resort experience out of nowhere if you have enough people to bully into doing the work.

He was unloading the gear, talking a mile a minute. The sound of his voice penetrated the log walls, setting my teeth on edge. I peeked out the window. It was camo heaven out there. Each of the men was hoisting some kind of duffle bag and stamping his feet, breathing in the alpine air, squinting heroically into the middle distance, fantasizing over the kills to be made in the days ahead. I just hoped no one expected me to cook any of it.

Uncle Vincent started in my direction.

"Cisco," he said grimly as he bashed through the door. "Smelling good!"

"Thanks." I glanced out at the group again. "Who's that?" I pointed at a familiar-looking elfin figure.

"Lara."

I looked again. There she was, surrounded on all sides by weapons of moose destruction.

"I didn't know she was going to be staying here," I said.

"Well," Uncle Vincent answered, "she showed up at the airport to meet her dad and then she insisted she come along." He lowered his voice and whispered, "I'll tell you about it later." He hollered out the door, "Grub's waiting!"

Ten L.A. yuppies jammed into the front hall. It crossed my mind that these men had never hunted before and what the hell were they thinking, wanting to start now? They flung their L.L. Bean gear in piles around the foyer. The room was a sea of plaid flannel.

"This is my nephew Cisco!" Uncle Vincent shouted at the group. He hauled me out of the kitchen by my arm. "Imported all the way from Vermont. Hell of a chef! Hell of a chef!"

Like him or hate him, Uncle Vincent was a positive thinker.

They looked at me. I could see the doubt, taste the disappointment.

One of the men said, "How old are you, kid?"

Uncle Vincent's hand tightened on my arm. "Eighteen," he said.

Lara's eyes widened. I tried not to look at her, but I couldn't help it.

I blinked. I was tall, so maybe that would help convince them. But the fact that I hadn't yet sprouted a whisker definitely wouldn't work in my favour. Shaving was nothing more than a distant dream. I tried to look mature—I straightened my shoulders and attempted eye contact.

No one seemed convinced.

"Sure smells good," Lara said, taking pity on me.

"Thank God for that," said the man who seemed to be her father. His name was Rick.

I prayed my voice wouldn't squeak or die on me. "Lunch is ready."

After that, no one spoke much. I kept ladling out bowl after bowl of soup. The bread was decimated in ten seconds. If it weren't for their well-fed girths, anyone would have thought these guys hadn't eaten for weeks.

Uncle Vincent pulled me aside after lunch to, as he said, "give me some background information." I now knew that on the drive up from the airport, Lara had confessed to her dad that she might have given him a slightly rosier picture of the lodge than it deserved, but her dad had seemed okay about it. Until they'd actually arrived, that is. But, hey, Vincent pointed out, Lara was his daughter. Dad wanted to make her happy, right? Okay, so she'd stretched the truth about the accommodations (considerably, if you ask me), but Vincent thought he was making it work (not a chance). Especially with my help.

After he left, I shook my head. From the expression on the

faces of the guests, I knew they weren't buying it, and there
was only so much homemade bread could do.

"Let's get you to your rooms," Uncle Vincent said.

I guessed he hoped lunch was going to soften them up,
because I couldn't imagine their reaction when they saw their
rooms. Late last night Uncle Vincent and I had hauled his liq-
uidation mattresses upstairs and each of the five bedrooms
other than Vincent's was now equipped with two. Not the
Beverly Hills Hilton, that was for sure. They forged their way
to their piles of gear and followed him upstairs. I watched
them go, completely expecting them to stampede right back
down the stairs when they saw the half-empty rooms and
the mattresses on the floor.

But they didn't. I don't know what Uncle Vincent said,
but they came back downstairs, grim-faced but calm. I was
thinking maybe Tony Robbins should move over, that Uncle
Vincent was going to take over the world as a salesman for
positive affirmations, when one of them said, "I could sue
your ass for this."

"Nonsense!" Uncle Vincent shouted. "Give it a chance!"

Lara had the grace to blush.

The men clenched their jaws. Not much joy in Mudville, if
you know what I mean.

Uncle Vincent cleared his throat and looked at me with
just a tinge of desperation. "We're heading out for some back-
country hiking this afternoon. Keep the home fires burning!"
The men just stared at us as if wondering whether or not we
might actually be dangerous. "You can't go anywhere until
tomorrow, so let's get out there and enjoy the mountains,"
Uncle Vincent pointed out.

Resignedly, the men milled around, hauling out some of
their cross-country ski gear. I went back to the kitchen and
started scrubbing pots.

"Want some help?" Lara asked. She was wearing camo pants and a khaki sweatshirt.

I flipped her a dishtowel. Who was I to say no? Figured it was the least she could do, after getting Uncle Vincent and me into this mess. She picked up a soup bowl and started drying it, without talking. If she was going to apologize, I hoped it would be soon.

She had a rope around her neck on which hung several keys, a carved swan and a dog tag. A real dog tag, that is—not the army version.

She caught me looking and said, "The swan was my nana's. My mom gave it to me after she died. I used to play with it all the time when I was a baby. The dog tag belonged to my dog. We just had to put him to sleep."

Too much information, my brain screamed. Condition red, condition red! Too much sharing. Not comfortable, not comfortable!

I swished the last coffee mug through the water.

Lara's eyes bored into the back of my neck. I rolled my head and flexed my shoulders.

"So, how'd you learn to cook, anyway?"

Many long hours in front of the TV watching all my favourite chefs while the rest of the guys bashed one another around on the football field. Many lonely nights making baklava while everyone else was out partying. Oh, the stories I could tell. Instead I just said, "Why do you ask so many questions?"

She put down the dishtowel. "Anyone ever tell you you've got a serious problem with anger?"

"What?"

"It's obvious. You can't talk without dripping anger all over the place."

"What are you? Some kind of California self-help wannabe?"

"I'm someone who knows a lot about pent-up anger. Which, by the way, is much healthier if you express it."

"Yeah, right. You could write a book on how to be passive-aggressive. Maybe you could ask your dad to write the introduction."

She turned red. "Not hostile at all, no kidding." Lara shuffled off to the door. "I think I'll go for a walk."

I slammed the dish cloth into the water and watched as it absorbed its weight in liquid and slowly sank to the bottom. You absorb enough shit without wringing yourself out, I thought, and look what happens.

18

By five o'clock it was pitch black. Lara was sitting in front of the fire, reading *The Lord of the Rings*. As if real life wasn't strange enough. I was in the kitchen spinning lettuce. I'd expected Uncle Vincent and the gang to be back by now, but the trail into the woods was a white ribbon of unblemished snow. It had started to snow again around three o'clock and hadn't stopped.

I stared at the veal chops for a while, then went and hauled up a case of the red wine Uncle Vincent had stashed in the cellar. I'd made more bread—homemade baguettes—and these were warming on the stovetop. I wanted to sit in front of the fire, but I didn't like the idea of talking to Lara. So I hung out in the kitchen and decided to make a cake.

I was just putting it in the oven when I heard barking. I checked out the window in time to see Uncle Vincent ski up to the front of the house. I wondered how the group had managed to keep up, and tried to remember what to do in the event of a heart attack.

The next two hours were chaos. The group parked themselves at the picnic table in front of the fireplace. Lara wedged
herself between her dad and a guy with slicked-back hair
and expensive gold jewellery. I carried in platters of food
and watched as everyone inhaled the veal chops, the salad,
the baguettes and the cake. It was gratifying to see, and I
relaxed when I realized that quality wasn't going to be that
important in the face of the appetite Uncle Vincent was creating. I had a moment of uncharacteristic optimism. Maybe
if he kept them busy enough no one would remember they
had threatened lawsuits.

"You're one fine cook, boy," said a man with a heavy Italian
accent named Cesare. "Reminds me of my mother's cooking.
Old-fashioned food with a twist."

"Thanks." It was after dinner, and I was sitting at the table
playing Monopoly with three of the other men. Lara wasn't
there. I wondered where she might have gone.

Lara's dad rolled the dice, landed on Park Place and put
up another hotel. I yawned. I had to get up early to start
breakfast. I planned on oatmeal brûlée with macerated ber-
ries and homemade cinnamon buns, so I thought I'd head
up to bed. Cesare was drinking heavily and acting weird. He
kept watching me as if trying to figure me out. He had a full
bottle of wine on the table beside him, his second. He was
starting to slur his words.

The group was winding down. Rick, having bought up all
of the Monopoly board, rubbed his hands together, yawned
widely enough for the rest of the room to see down his throat
to his spleen and announced he was hitting the sack.

I put away the last of the booze, feeling a little like Dustin
Hoffman in *The Graduate* when he looks forlornly at all the
adults in his life and just doesn't get where they're coming

from. As I shelved the half-empty bottles, thinking that these guys sure could drink, Uncle Vincent cornered me in the kitchen.

"Good job there, Cisco." He slapped me on the back. "I think we've got them hooked!" He'd been drinking too. He winked, then he and his delusions headed for the stairs. "See you in the morning."

I sat at the kitchen table and stared at the night sky.

I don't like spending too much time alone with crazy angst-ridden thoughts. I mean, life is what it is. There's no point in trying to figure it out. Adults aren't much further ahead than kids, as far as I can see. I mean, look at Rocky. Where did he get off marrying Delta, having three kids and then changing his mind? You can be confused about a lot of things—like how we screw up the environment, like how people can drive gas-guzzling SUVs, or even whether we should legalize pot—but how can you be confused about something like that? I didn't like these thoughts, so I shoved them aside. I reviewed my mental checklist of safe topics and came up with one. Tomorrow's menu. Trouble is, after that, it got kind of scary. I didn't have much left that I wanted to think about.

"Hey," a soft voice said at my side.

I jumped. It was Lara.

"Sorry if I scared you," she said.

"Don't worry about it."

"Couldn't sleep," she said. "That's the problem with sharing a room with my dad. He snores like a boxer with a broken nose. Plus, I've had trouble sleeping ever since I was little."

"So what's your dad going to do?"

"I think they're going to try to find another place to stay. A couple of the guys were talking and said there was no way they were paying $250 bucks a night for this dump. I'm sorry, Cisco."

I thought of Uncle Vincent saying he thought they were hooked. I actually got a lump in my throat.

Lara reached over and patted my arm. "Like I said, I'm sorry. I guess I really screwed up. But I didn't realize there weren't any beds upstairs, for Pete's sake."

In spite of the fact that I felt like crying, I almost laughed.

"Poor Vincent," I said.

Lara shook her head thoughtfully. "Maybe he should rethink his approach. I mean, there are people out there who really want this kind of vacation."

"Yeah, right."

"I mean it. People pay big bucks to sleep in tents on the bank of the Amazon River. This looks positively luxurious next to that. Or there are Outward Bound groups. Survivalists. That sort of thing."

I sighed.

Lara leaned back. "Plus there are bigger problems in the world," she said.

"Yeah," I answered solemnly, thinking of Mr. Patterson and Rocky. "You have a point there."

"Take my mom. After I left in the fall, she had a breakdown. Now she's gone in for a facelift. At forty."

"No shit?"

"Yeah. She discovered a line beside her nose. Panicked. My dad says she's nuts."

"What do you think?"

"I think she's pathetic."

"How can you say that? She's your mom, after all."

Lara sighed and rubbed her feet. "You really can't believe the kind of crap that goes on where I live. All the moms are getting themselves cut-and-pasted for their fortieth birthdays. I mean, really. I could look at it and think my life's going to be washed up by twenty-five. I've got friends who asked for boob jobs at sixteen." Lara crossed her arms over her chest protectively. "At least you come from someplace real." She gave me a spooky, white-face look. "So," Lara said. "Your turn. Why aren't you in Vermont? You never did tell me what you are doing stuck way out here." She moved away from the window and picked at the parsley I had stuck in a glass of water on the counter. She picked a sprig and ate it.

I watched her, fascinated. No one ever did that.

"I don't like to talk about it," I said.

"Why not?"

Because, I almost shrieked at her, *I don't like to* think *about it.* "Don't know," I said.

"Sure you do."

"Hey." I hate it when someone pushes me to talk. It has the opposite effect.

"All right." She held up her hand, then pinched off another piece of parsley and sucked on it while she studied me. "Let's get back to where you learned to cook."

"Mostly from myself. My mom was out a lot. So I learned out of self-preservation. But I kind of liked it, so I kept at it. Now my whole family's vegetarian except for me."

"Lots of my friends are vegetarian. I think it's a rite of passage or something." She paused, then asked, "So you ever going to tell me why you're here?"

There was Mr. Patterson again—his hospital gown flapping as he danced a jig across the room. He was barefoot, totally without rhythm and in grave danger of exposing his bony old rump. I shook my head, trying to dislodge him.

Lara watched me strangely. "You okay?"

"I got into some trouble back in Vermont," I said. I cleared my throat, took a breath. This was hard. Truly hard. I hadn't talked about this to anyone.

"What kind of trouble?"

"Never mind." I couldn't do it. Couldn't go through with it. Talking about it would make it seem too real, too true. Mr. Patterson shook his head reprovingly. It's hard to think you've disappointed anyone, especially a comatose old man who seems to enjoy teleporting himself into your head.

"I really thought my dad would get over the shock," Lara said, changing the subject. "I just wanted to shake him up a little. He thinks he can control everything."

"Well, Lara. I think he can control whether or not he sticks around. Unfortunately."

"I could try talking to him," Lara said. "Not that it'll do much good. He likes things new and fresh. Just ask my mom."

"It sure is a mess," I said.

Lara pushed off from the counter and sat down. "You got any wine?"

I checked her out. She seemed serious enough. "You're not old enough."

"You asking for I.D.?"

"No." God, no. Life was embarrassing enough without being seen as some kind of morality cop.

"So where's the wine?"

I got a bottle from the cupboard. It was half full. "What's with that Cesare, anyhow?"

"Oh, him." Lara picked up the bottle and carried it to the counter, where she put it down. She lifted a glass from the dish rack and turned to look at me. "Want some?"

"Yeah," I said, then wondered whose voice was coming out of my mouth.

Lara put a half-full glass in front of me. "I'm going to be sixteen," she said. "Next week." She lifted her glass. "Let's drink to birthdays without boob jobs."

We clinked. I sipped the wine. Lara drank quietly, staring out the window.

"I don't much like my father," she said.

"Why not?"

"The real reason my parents are getting a divorce is that he's got someone else. My mom only *thinks* it's because she's not young enough."

"Hmm," I said.

She gave me a puzzled look. "Don't you think that sucks?"

"I don't know. Shit happens. What's your dad say?"

"He doesn't really talk about it. I don't think that's the real reason, actually. I think he's kind of fed up."

"My dad's gay."

There. I'd said it. I hadn't even known I was going to say it. I hadn't told anyone except Karen, and immediately after that I'd had regrets. I put the wine down and wished I had just shut up. Any second now I was going to spew out chunks of undigested anger.

Lara looked at me over the rim of her glass.

"Here," she said, holding out the bottle. "Have some more."

She refilled my glass and I drank it down in one gulp, felt a good kind of burn.

Lara sipped her wine and smiled. "So what are you scared of?"

"*Say what?*" I was winding down a little. Enjoying the buzz.

"You. You're so choked, I'm surprised you can breathe."

The tension was back, lodged like a giant airbag in my chest, making breathing pretty darn hard.

She edged her chair a little closer to mine. I skittered away. I was petrified. I didn't want to be that close to her in case she put a spell over me and made me tell her things I wasn't planning on telling anyone, ever—like how angry I felt when I tackled Mr. Patterson, or how I was really scared that he might die, or even that part of me wanted an avalanche to take out Ralph Brewster. She was leaning forward now, breathing softly,

I could feel little, tickly puffs wafting over my cheek. It took every ounce of willpower I possessed to keep from bolting for the door.

Gorgeous whimpered in her sleep, twitching and half-opening her eyes. She looked like my stomach felt. I hiccuped.

"There's a plant I read about," Lara said. "A type of gourd or something. It's from the desert." She paused, took a sip of wine and continued. "I read that it lived in a glass display case for seven years without soil or water. And every year it sent out some little shoots, checking to see if it was raining yet. When nothing happened, it dried up again until the next year. Ya gotta love something like that." She twiddled with the little pot of rosemary I had picked up in the grocery store, as if assessing its spell potential. "Well," she said, "better get some sleep."

Then she leaned over and kissed me, starting a little bonfire in the groin area. I couldn't even look at her. I focused on the empty wine bottle instead. She tasted like parsley.

I didn't kiss her back.

She pulled away, watched me with her wide, questioning eyes, then stood up and wafted out of the room, touching my shoulder on her way by.

A soft, silvery cloud drifted across the sky and I concentrated on whether or not it would hit the moon. I stared at her empty chair.

Rocky used to come into my room at night, after everyone was in bed. I heard him, even though I always pretended to be asleep. He'd hang up my clothes, adjust the dinosaurs I kept on my dresser, straighten my blankets. Sometimes he'd sit in the chair at my window. I'd pretend he wasn't there. I'd try as hard as I could to fall asleep.

But I knew he was there, all right. Sometimes he'd stay all night. I'd watch him through slitted eyes, watching me.

I never knew just what it was he was doing there or what he wanted from me. Now, though, it occurred to me that he might have been running away from Delta. Wondering about me. Wondering just exactly how things had gotten so screwed up. Maybe trying to figure stuff out. Why he chose my room is anybody's guess. Maybe he took some sort of comfort in watching me sleep. Who knows?

My first kiss and it came with all kinds of accompanying voices for my listening pleasure. *So that wasn't so scary now, was it?* came the timid voice that might have just wondered how I was going to feel about this whole sex thing after Rocky's somewhat surprising revelation. *Go for it,* snarled a rather animal-like creature that was squatting just behind the gonads. *So shut up everybody,* I commanded, shoving myself out of my seat and swirling Lara's glass and mine in soapy water. I was scared. Only I didn't exactly know what I was scared of. Of what might happen to Mr. P? How I felt about Rocky? Was it even possible I might turn out like he did? All my life people had told me that I was just like my dad. Looked like him. Sounded like him. I was hit with an idea. That French singer who said, *"Je ne regrette rien"* didn't know diddly.

All this bullshit about not having regrets is just that, bullshit. You can't be human and not have regrets. I could list my regrets. I regretted putting Mr. P in a coma. I regretted not telling Lonigan and his mother exactly what I thought of them. I regretted not telling Rocky what a crap job he'd made of his and everyone else's life. I regretted not asking Rocky what he wanted all those nights he sat in my room.

And right up there on my top-ten list was a new one. I regretted not kissing Lara back when I had the chance.

19

The next morning my mouth felt like scraped, burned toast. I woke too late to start the cinnamon buns, so I made pancakes instead. No one even noticed. The group was bleary eyed and pretzel-shaped from sleeping on mattresses on the floor. Their patience had clearly worn as thin as Lara's father's hair. I knew Uncle Vincent's goose was cooked, and wondered if he had a plan B now that he had the tax department *and* a potential lawsuit to deal with.

Cesare slurped his coffee as if his lips were Novocained. Rick drummed his fingers on the table. I slapped a short stack in front of him, which he barely noticed. Uncle Vincent had already decamped to the front hall, where he was throwing gear into a pile to take out to the van. I followed, carrying a cup of coffee, which I held out to him.

"Thanks, Cisco," Uncle Vincent said as he paused in his labours. He cupped the steaming coffee in two hands. He shook his head, his voice wounded. "Rick just told me they want to get out of here before noon. I just don't get it. Who wouldn't like it here?"

So they really were going. I checked my uncle out. He truly didn't get it. You gotta respect a person with that much optimism.

"I thought it was going all right," I ventured.

"Yeah. Well, I guess not." He sighed. "Sorry, Cisco. Looks like I'm going to have to pay you back later."

"Fuggedaboudit," I said.

He almost smiled, then resumed hurling expensive equipment into a giant pile.

I started back to the kitchen. It occurred to me that if Uncle Vincent had to sell his ranch, I'd get to go home sooner. That expression "Be careful what you wish for" crossed my mind.

Back in the kitchen, Rick was mopping his plate with his last forkful of pancake.

"Hey, kid," he said when I walked in, "got any more of these?" He gestured at his empty plate.

I ladled some batter onto the griddle and stared at the bubbles popping to the surface.

Behind me, Rick said, "Only good thing about this whole damn place is your cooking, kid."

I didn't want to like him for that, but I did. Lara came down just as the others were fighting over the one bathroom.

"Pancakes?" I asked, feeling kind of shy.

"Sure." She sat down, poured herself some coffee, stared at me.

I handed her a plate.

I didn't know what to say, so I fiddled with the reception on Uncle Vincent's transistor. A distant-sounding voice announced I was listening to CBC/Radio-Canada and I jumped, startled. Lara smiled at me over her pancakes. Mona Lisa with syrup stuck to her chin.

"Is that what I think it is?" she asked, cocking her head and listening to the music.

I dragged my attention away from her and listened.

"Oh my God," she said. "It is. It's 'Hello Muddah, Hello Faddah', in Yiddish. This is some kind of country."

"Yeah," I said, wondering how she knew it was Yiddish.

"My mom's Jewish," she said, as if she had read my mind. Then, as if thinking about her mom made her sad, she shoved the pancakes aside and gulped at her coffee. "I'm sorry we're leaving today," she said. "I asked my dad to stay, but all the others want to go. They got some last-minute deal at another place twenty miles away."

"Yeah, well."

"Too bad. Just when you were loosening up."

"Hey," I said.

She smiled. "Guess what?"

I shrugged.

"One guess," she encouraged. I shook my head. "Or I'll take it back about loosening up."

I started scraping the dried bits of pancake batter off the griddle. She was going to make me wait.

"Cesare wants to stay behind so he can learn the Yiddish words to 'Hello Muddah, Hello Faddah.'"

She rolled her eyes. "Very funny. But not so crazy."

I leaned on the counter and tossed my spatula into the sink, splashing water on the floor.

"Cesare likes your cooking."

"Well, thanks." I knew that. He'd eaten more than anyone else.

"He thinks you've got something special. Says he can't stand all the New Age foodie crap he gets served in L.A. Says your stuff takes him back to Minneapolis when he was a kid."

"A big Italian momma. That's me."

"It think it's the aesthetic." She smiled, pleased at her use of a big word. "He likes the idea of throwback cuisine."

NANCY BELGUE | 149

"Throwback cuisine?"

"That's what he said. I eavesdropped last night after I went up to bed. I'm an expert at it. It's the only way I ever find out what's happening in my house—"

"So, like I said," I interrupted, "throwback cuisine?"

"Yeah. Some kind of time-warp TV show about old-fashioned cooking. He smells a hit. Says he's a visionary. People want to travel back to when things are safer. Can't do it for real, but sure can do it with their food. Says he thinks you might be the man."

"What do you mean?"

"He's a producer for the Good Eating Channel. He wants to talk to you about maybe doing a show."

"What?"

"Like I said."

"No way."

"That so hard to believe?"

It was, actually. Nothing good ever happens to me. At least nothing ever had before. Maybe I had to thank Delta and Rocky for all their retro influences after all.

"I heard him telling my dad he was going to speak to you before they left. See if you wanted to come down to L.A. for a screen test or something."

"You're not serious."

"Couldn't be more."

"Me?"

"He said you could be America's answer to Jamie Oliver. He said—" she stopped. Footsteps thundered down the stairs. "Well, I guess I'll let him tell you what he said."

She resumed eating while I just stared at the door to the kitchen. Voices rose and fell in the front hallway. Dogs barked. Uncle Vincent's bellow could be heard above it all.

"DOWN, Gorgeous!"

Clearly he had rebounded philosophically from the entire fiasco. Lara finished her breakfast and stood up.

"Lara." I wanted to tell her something. But, I wasn't quite sure what to say. I have perfected the art of not making conversation.

She nodded as if she understood perfectly. When she brushed her lips over mine, I grabbed her arms and put some pressure into it. She broke away, smiled like she was a hundred years older than I was, then headed for the door.

Behind me, the crazy strains of "Hello Muddah, Hello Faddah," continued unabated.

The door opened and Cesare was standing there. He was unshaven and smelled of alcohol, but his eyes were intense. I could see the wheeler-dealer behind the drunk.

"Hey, kid," he said, gesturing for me to sit down. I was grateful that Lara had given me advance warning about what he wanted to say. "You ever thought about cooking on TV?"

"Can't say that I have."

"I got a hunch about you, kid. You're telegenic. You can cook. I'm thinking of putting you into a situation. You interested in exploring a little situation with me?"

"Situation?" I had to admit, being on TV sounded like an interesting proposition.

"Come to L.A. Do a test. Talk to some people. I'm good at spotting talent. I'll get in touch with your parents."

"Uh, no." The mention of parents shocked me into reality. No. No. No. He wouldn't want anything to do with me if he knew why I was here. I thought of Mr. Patterson. *Glug, glug, glug* percolated the sick feeling in my gut.

"Whaddaya mean no?" He leaned forward.

I could smell his mouthwash mingled with last night's bourbon.

"I couldn't. Really."

He slapped the table. Stood up. Handed me his card. "You think it over, kid. Call me if you change your mind."

I took his card. Yankee Noodle Dandy Productions. "Cute," I said.

"What's that?" He turned at the door, squinted as if sizing me up.

I smiled. Saluted with his card, then stuffed it in my pocket. He gave me a sour look and went into the hall.

As everyone streamed out to the van, Lara passed by me and squeezed my left buttock, making me jump. I headed outside last, looking for her, and spotted her in the front seat of the van. She winked at me. I raised my hand in salute. Then they were gone.

Back in the kitchen I picked up the phone and then put it down. I stared at it.

I hadn't talked to anyone from home in a few days. I picked it up. Put it down again.

What if Mr. Patterson didn't wake up? This was one of the things on the list that I tried not to think about. And I'd been successful, if you didn't count my dreams.

I hate it when people go on about their dreams, like anyone else really cares. But I'd had some real doozies since I'd been at Treetop. Mostly I'd been chased around a lot by skinny old men carrying big sticks. It was all pretty Freudian, even I recognized that. Dreams betray the subconscious, Delta says. Betray is right. The content of my dreams was not PG.

So, Lara, I thought. If you really want to know what I'm scared of, how about this. It was something I didn't want to admit even to myself. Was it possible I could turn out to be like Rocky? Even Delta said I was just like my father. My voice sounded so much like his, people couldn't tell us apart on the phone. We walked alike. Looked alike. Sounded alike, for God's sake. Where did he end and I begin? What if I was like him in other ways too? I didn't think so, I liked girls okay, especially Lara—but what if I was wrong? What if I really didn't know which side of the fence I was on? Just like Rocky.

What if I didn't figure it out until it was too late? Just like Rocky.

My hand started to shake. I wanted to break something and the nearest thing was Uncle Vincent's ancient radio. I picked it up and tested the heft. Drew my arm back and got ready to hurl it. The phone rang and like a fighter that was down for the count and trying to throw one last punch, I let that transistor radio fly at the window, sending splinters of glass into orbit and knocking the parsley off the windowsill and into the sink.

The phone shrilled again and I stared at it like it was a foreign object that had somehow landed in this kitchen far, far away.

And I just knew. It wasn't going to be good news.

20

"Hello?"

"Cisco. Hi." It was Delta. Her voice was croaky.

"Is everyone okay?"

"Oh, Cisco."

"What's wrong?"

"It's Mr. Patterson."

I knew it. In the back of my mind, I'd always known this day was going to come. I twirled the phone cord around my finger, cutting off the circulation. I stared at the red tip, watched it pulsate. Made me think of *ET*.

"Cisco?"

"Yeah, I'm here."

"I just heard. Mr. Patterson died early this morning."

I shut my eyes, let the phone cord drop, released the blood flow to my finger. "What happened?" I asked.

"He just never regained consciousness. His heart gave out."

I opened my eyes. "What's going to happen now?"

"I don't know. Rick says they're going to do an autopsy. He

says you better come home. Is Uncle Vincent there?"

"He's gone into town."

"Why aren't you at school?"

"It's a long story."

I kept seeing Mr. Patterson's faded blue eyes staring at me from behind his old-man glasses. I guess I was never going to be able to tell him I was sorry, which seemed like the only thing I really wanted to do any more.

"What do you mean?" Delta's voice had taken on an edge, like a newly sharpened carving knife.

"Snow day." I figured I'd leave the rest of the story for another time.

She sighed. I heard whispering, then she said, "Rocky wants to talk to you." She passed him the phone.

"Son?"

My head started to pound. "Yeah?"

"Look, this wasn't your fault, but we think you'd better come home. I'm booking you a flight for tomorrow. We need to get you back here." Rocky sounded firm and in charge. *This is all your fault*, I wanted to scream at him.

"Cisco?" It was Delta again. "Cisco?"

"Yeah, I'm here."

"Tell Vincent to call the minute he gets back."

"Yeah, sure."

"Are you going to be all right?"

"Yeah." I hung up.

Mr. Patterson. Dead. I could hardly take it in. Had I killed him? It truly didn't seem possible. I thought back to that day. All I'd done was try to take away his gun. How had things gotten so screwed up? A nervous type of energy zapped through my ganglia, making sitting still impossible. I wanted to scream, break more things.

The phone rang again and I didn't answer it. A blast of cold air hit me in the face and I realized that there was a north wind coming in the broken windowpane. I found a piece of cardboard and some duct tape, and tried to cover the hole. It helped a little but not much. The cold oozed out from around the cardboard and penetrated the kitchen. I felt something wet and looked down. My hand was covered in blood. I must have cut my wrist on a piece of glass. I watched the blood bubble up out of the cut the way I'd watched the bubbles break through the surface of the pancake batter. I picked the parsley out of the sink and set it on the counter, accidentally smearing some blood on the sink. The clay pot was cracked but still holding together.

The phone rang again. I let it ring.

It was quiet in the house with everyone gone. Even the dogs had disappeared. I thought about hiking up to Virgil's empty cabin and staying there for the rest of my life. It seemed like the simplest thing to do. No one would miss me and I would miss no one. Just like Simon and Garfunkel said. *I am a rock.*

I started to cry. I didn't like to think of Mr. Patterson dead in his hospital room with no one but that doughy daughter-in-law to see him on his way. I was really sorry I'd tackled him that day—maybe I should have let him blast O'Reilly and Lester. I shook my head and tried to think it through, but couldn't. All I could see was Mr. Patterson's bony knuckles lying on the white bedsheet.

The phone rang again, but this time someone picked it up. I heard voices.

Then Uncle Vincent was standing in the door to the kitchen. He looked around, zeroed in on the broken window, followed the trail of blood to my wrist.

He crossed the kitchen in three steps. Then he had me in his arms, like I was one of the twins' rag dolls.

"It's gonna be okay, Cisco. You hear your Uncle Vincent? It's gonna be okay."

21

"The findings of the autopsy are conclusive," Rocky said.

Delta reached for my hand, holding it gently because my wrist was still bandaged. On the other side, Rocky patted my shoulder. Uncle Vincent grunted in the chair in front of the fireplace.

"Heart failure," Rocky said.

I stared at my shoes. I tried to get a direct line to Mr. Patterson—who had decided to make his intrusion into my life permanent—to tell him I was really sorry the way things had turned out, but my head was fuzzy. The latest shrink was the real deal and he was big on handing out meds. I'd been back in Lovell for two weeks. It seemed like two years.

"However," Rocky continued, "the family is considering a civil suit—"

Did everyone stop breathing? The room was without sound, the way underground caves are without light.

"—but we'll cross that bridge when we come to it."

Stupid cow, muttered Mr. Patterson. *It's his wife's fault. That son of mine never did have any gumption.* I tried to shrug him away. Ever since that day in the hospital, he'd been hanging around in my head, but since his death he'd moved in. It made me think about heaven and hell. Was Mr. Patterson up in space somewhere talking it over with God, letting him know that he'd been a good guy, even if he'd never wanted to hand out Halloween treats to little kids. Would that nasty streak be enough to keep him out of heaven? Was God like the judge, shuffling papers and going on about extenuating circumstances and corroborating evidence? So you were a lousy father, but you never broke a law. Oh, you hated children, but you never contributed to tooth rot. You were a hard worker, but you never had any joy. Mr. Patterson would probably rather spend eternity telling people off than listening to a bunch of nonsense like that. I listened for his voice, but he was momentarily quiet.

Rocky put his arm around me. I stiffened, then forced myself to relax. The meds did kind of smooth out the rough edges—I had to give them that.

I wasn't even offended that Delta had made a vegetarian buffet.

Uncle Vincent, who had flown back with me because he doubted my cut wrist was a total accident, ate with his usual gusto. Nothing seemed to dim his appetite. Not even Delta's tofu shish kebabs.

The twins leaned against me, one on either side. I liked their weight, liked their smell. The house was overheated in the January cold. I was having re-entry problems. In fact, I think it would be fair to say I was having problems, period. I picked up a pair of scissors and stared at the blades. Delta removed them gently from my fingers and the twins disappeared. The voices in the kitchen didn't seem human, they seemed like echoes.

I shovelled in some of the kebab just to keep Delta happy. When Ralph appeared to drive my father back to Stowe and Delta brought him in for a cup of herbal tea, I saw him touch my father's hand tenderly. Made me sick. I took off for my room. I lay on my bed and thought about Lara. I had thought about Lara a lot since I'd been back. I'd even called information and gotten her Aunt Annie's phone number in case I ever screwed up the courage to call her. I wondered if she ever thought about me. I wondered how her mother's facelift had gone. I reached into my pocket and took out the crumpled scrap of paper I'd written her phone number on. I carried it everywhere, like it was a talisman that could ward off evil spirits. Hear that, Mr. Patterson? I liked to look at the number, pretend I didn't speak or read English and imagine what it would mean to me if I didn't associate it with big, see-through eyes and parsley breath.

Uncle Vincent loomed in my doorway. He seemed even bigger in this house than he did in the mountains, where the peaks kind of put him in perspective. He'd stuck around longer than he'd planned. I couldn't figure out why. Maybe it was easier for him to meddle in my problems than solve his own, I thought nastily. He caught me looking at Lara's phone number, which I jammed into a sweaty ball in my palm, but he didn't say anything.

"How's it going?"

He was a lot quieter here too. The household kind of numbed everyone.

"Great."

"So what are you going to do now?"

"Good question." I didn't look forward to returning to school.

"You could always come back and live with me."

I heard a murmuring, like the sound of melting snow. I cocked an ear. Mr. Patterson was about to weigh in with his opinion.

"Yeah," Uncle Vincent continued. "You could finish the year up in Canada, like you planned."

I shifted onto my side and stared right at him. He stared back, unafraid. Met my eyes in a way Rocky hadn't done for some time. I liked that. "The year's shot anyway," I pointed out.

"Not necessarily," Uncle Vincent said. "You've only missed a few weeks. Smart kid like you. You could make it up in no time. Think about it." He got up and headed for the hall. "And call that girl," he said, looking at the paper in my hand. "Do you good."

Downstairs, the twins started yelling at each other and the smell of coffee trailed up the hall and into my room. An icicle outside released its grip on the eaves and crashed to the ground. In six months it would be spring. I looked at the numbers again like they were some kind of magical code to a secret vault and wondered where Lara was at that very moment. Mr. Patterson whispered something in my ear. *Hey, kid,* he said cheerily.

I swung my legs over the side of the bed. Maybe I would call her.

Do it, Mr. Patterson said encouragingly.

I went into the hall. There was a phone in Delta's bedroom. From the hall window, I could see the twins outside flailing away in an attempt to make snow angels.

Rocky's voice carried up the stairs.

"I'm worried about him, Delta."

"Give him time."

"Hell, let him come back to the ranch with me," Uncle Vincent said.

I sat down on the top stair. This was interesting.

"Is he talking to the doctor?"

"I don't know. The doctor says they're making progress. He can't tell me any more than that."

"Why don't you invite him to spend the weekend with us in Stowe, Rocky?"

I craned my neck. Ralph Brewster was still here. My gut gurgled. I scowled at Mr. Patterson, who was hovering politely over my shoulder.

"I don't think he's ready for that."

"He's got to get used to the idea. Maybe that's exactly what he needs."

"Maybe *I'm* not ready, then," Rocky said.

Mr. Patterson clucked at my elbow. He was lying on the ground now, leaning his wrinkled chin on his hand.

I stood up. Like any of them had any idea what I needed. I went into Delta's room, grabbed the portable phone out of its receiver and headed back to my room.

"Lara?" I said when she answered. She sounded sleepy, and I remembered it was three hours earlier on the West Coast.

I wanted to hang up. My voice caught in my throat and I coughed.

"Cisco!" She was awake now.

"Hi." I cleared my throat. Mr. Patterson floated by and perched on the dresser, right on top of my Julia Child collection.

"What's going on? Where have you been?"

So I told her. I told her about Mr. Patterson, who, at the mention of his name, waved at me. He was a much cheerier ghost than he had been a person. Lara listened without inter-rupting. I once heard an expression about how some people listen with their eyes, and that's what I imagined Lara doing.

When I was done talking, Lara said, "You didn't do any-thing wrong."

I started to cry again. Mr. Patterson clucked disapprovingly, and I tried to suck it up, be a man, but the tears just kept on flowing.

Lara didn't say anything else. She let me sob. It was weirdly companionable. Mr. Patterson started thumbing through *The Art of French Cooking*, and my sobs turned into chuckles. If I was going to be haunted, I guessed it was nice to have a ghost that at least tried to share my interests.

"I'm going to L.A. for a visit during March break," Lara said. "Why don't you come out too? It might be good for you to get away from everybody. We could hang around, go surfing."

"Surfing?"

"Just seeing if you were paying attention."

"I can't come out there."

"You can if you want to."

"How's your mom?" I asked, changing the subject.

"Don't know. Talked to her yesterday. She still has bandages. I guess she's fine." Lara paused. "Cisco?"

"Yeah?"

"That guy, Cesare? He really was serious about you. He wants to talk to you. My dad says he's been calling your uncle's place looking for you. Now I know why he can't find you. Do you mind if I give him your phone number?"

"I don't know." I thought of Cesare sizing me up like a fresh soufflé. Mr. Patterson looked up from Julia and raised an eyebrow.

"He says he can't stop thinking about this idea he has and now he's got a concept. Something about shooting it at your uncle's cabin. He likes the idea of range cooking. I don't know. But I thought maybe—" She stopped again.

I scraped at the frost on my window. They all said I could go back to school, but I couldn't do it. Uncle Vincent's cabin seemed like a vast improvement over Lovell. A place where everybody knows your name is not all it's cracked up to be.

"I thought maybe this could help out your uncle," Lara finished.

I was tired now. "I'll think about it."

"Remember, Cisco," Lara said. "None of this is your fault."

I nodded, felt the hard ball in my chest expand again, and hung up the phone.

Mr. Patterson fluttered around the room like a bat wanting to escape.

"Go!" I shouted at him. "So go, already! Who asked you to set up housekeeping in my room?" I tried to open the window but couldn't, and he just kept fluttering around, all agitated. I picked up my Julia Child and threw it. The window broke with a satisfying crunch and sent a spray of glass flying in all directions. Instead of exiting, Mr. Patterson settled comfortably on the end of my bed and shook his head.

I'd gotten it wrong again.

Footsteps pounded up the stairs and the next thing I knew, Rocky, Delta, Uncle Vincent and even Ralph Brewster were standing in the doorway surveying the splintered window and the shards of glass that glinted nastily from the floor.

"Son?" Rocky picked his way across the room. "Are you all right?"

So. What do you say? *Of course I'm all right. I was just trying to open the window so the ghost of Mr. Patterson could escape.*

Rocky sat on the bed. He gestured at the others to go away. Delta started forward as if to say, *Hey, I'm not going anywhere,* but stopped when Rocky said, "I want to talk to Cisco." Mr. Patterson settled in like this was exactly what he'd planned all along. The others backed out of the room and Delta closed the door with a soft *click.* Rocky turned and looked at me.

"I guess," he said, "that it's time you and I had a talk."

22

"You can ask me anything you want," Rocky said.

Mr. Patterson nodded encouragingly at me.

"I don't have any questions." I moved away, picking up bits of glass, stuffed a pillow in the window.

"I don't blame you for being angry," Rocky said. "It's normal."

"Nothing about this situation is normal."

"Well, that's true. All I know is that nothing's changed about how I feel about you. You're still my son. I love you."

"I don't even know who you are."

"Of course you do."

"Why didn't you come after me the day I got suspended from school? That fight wasn't my fault."

"I'm sorry about that. I was raw too. I was letting my own feelings get in the way of my obligations to you. This hasn't been easy for me."

"So why did you do it?" I yelled. Then I stopped, clamped down on the anger. I wasn't going to give in to it. He wasn't going to make me.

"Cisco—"

Rocky was pale. He'd lost weight. He didn't look too good. I didn't want to be noticing any of that.

"—it got to the point that I couldn't be that other person any more. I had to do something about my life."

"So what about us?"

"I'm still here for you. Just because I've finally admitted who I am doesn't mean I can't be your father."

"It's not the same."

"Can't it be even better? Now that you know the truth, I can stop pretending."

I shook my head. Rocky put his arm on my shoulder, and I shrugged it off. "How could you not have known?" I asked.

Rocky rubbed his hand over his eyes. They were bloodshot. I glanced away.

"I didn't want to know," he said finally. "I wanted a family. I wanted a life that I considered to be normal. I loved your mother. I still do. But this other thing, it's stronger than I realized." He was watching me now. "Cisco," he said quietly, "are you wondering about yourself?"

"No!" I screamed at him.

"Because that would be normal."

I was sick of the word *normal*. I was sick of the words *talk to me*. I was just plain sick of it all. I flopped back on the bed and turned to the wall.

"Careful you don't cut yourself, son," Rocky said. He stood up and started picking up the pieces.

"Just get out of here," I said.

"I want you to remember one thing. I love you."

I grunted. Rocky kept picking up broken glass. I heard it tinkle into the wastebasket, then he shut the door.

I took stock. Right at that moment I hated my father. I wasn't going to go back to Lovell District High School, no matter what. Everyone thought I was going crazy. And my only friend was a dead senior citizen who in life had seriously hated kids. It was pretty pathetic.

One thing Rocky had said stuck with me. Was I afraid of being like him? I thought of Lara, thought of her kissing me and decided to concentrate on that. Paris and India poked their heads in the door. Of my entire family, they were the only ones who didn't make me angry.

"Hi, Cisco," Paris said.

"Watch for glass," I told her.

"We brought the vacuum," India said, kicking the door wider and pulling the vacuum into the room. "Delta told us to clean up for you."

I watched while my sisters hoovered up my mess. Mr. Patterson smiled a gummy smile, and I picked up the paper with Lara's number one more time.

"Cisco," yelled Delta.

I gestured to India to turn off the vacuum. "Yeah?"

"Karen's here."

Boom ba da boom ba da boom boom boom went my heart. I stood up and smoothed the back of my hair where it separates into two halves and makes me look bald. I had a premonition of things to come and could see myself when I was Mr. Patterson's age—old, bald and permanently pissed off.

India gave me a weird look as I stepped over the vacuum and headed downstairs. Karen was in the foyer, staring up at me. She smiled when I raised my hand.

"Let's go for a walk," I said.

She nodded, and I pulled on my coat. The faces of Rocky, Delta and Uncle Vincent watched me from the kitchen table. Rocky, guilty. Delta, worried. Uncle Vincent, pleased.

Karen took my arm as we headed down the walk. "Want to go to the bridge?"

"Aren't you afraid I might throw myself off?"

"Hell, no."

I smiled. "Karen, it's good to see you again."

"Thanks, Cisco. Where've you been? I've called a bunch of times."

"They don't like to let me out of their sight."

"I heard about that. You really try to kill yourself?"

No, I'd just been busy breaking windows. I guess it's all in how it looks, and I hadn't really bothered to tell anyone anything different. "No."

She punched my arm. "I heard Patterson's son is threatening to sue."

"Yeah."

"What for?"

"Who knows? Assault, wrongful death."

"He won't. Even Lonigan says it wasn't your fault."

"Yeah?" That was news to me.

"As if anyone would believe *him*."

"Thanks, Karen. Sometimes you're just such a comfort."

"Any time." She grinned.

The streets were empty. It was cold and wintery. A fresh dump of snow had landed on Lovell the night before. I guessed it was going to be a long winter, with no chance of an early thaw. Karen's breath was silvery white, and over my shoulder I could hear Mr. Patterson puffing along behind me, trying to keep up. I thought ghosts would just fly along, but not Mr. Patterson. He was making a big production out of keeping up. I started to slow my pace, then thought, *what the hell am I doing?*

"I actually came to say goodbye," Karen said.

I tuned back into the conversation that I realized had been going on without me. "Where are you going?"

"I knew you weren't listening. Cisco, I'm heading out west. To L.A."

"You don't look much like an L.A. person to me."

"You gotta get over these ideas, Cisco. Not everyone in L.A. is some kind of a phoney."

"I guess." I thought of Lara. "Yeah, I guess."

"All the stuff that's happened to you has made me realize something. You can sit around waiting for shit to happen or you can go out and kick up some of your own. So I owe you one."

"Glad to help."

"What about you? What are you going to do?"

"Don't know."

"Well, it seems to me you should know. You should at least think about it. Lying around pretending to be depressed isn't going to get you anywhere."

"Hey."

"No, you gotta listen to me, Cisco. So your old man comes home one day and says he's gay. Big deal. I mean, not to be insensitive or anything, but he's still here, isn't he? He's still around. At least he didn't die, or run off and leave you."

"You don't get it."

"I get it. Believe me, I get it." She stopped and grabbed my arm, turned me to look at her, square in the face.

Karen always did have trouble keeping her mouth shut. It was one of the things I liked about her. Until this moment. I knew she was about to tell me things I didn't want to hear.

"So you're probably wondering about girls, huh?"

"Shut up."

"No. I'm leaving Lovell anyway, so if you wind up hating me, that's going to be too bad, but at least I won't be seeing you every day. So, I'm going to tell you this whether you want to hear it or not. All your life everyone's told you that you're the spitting image of your father. Like you're a clone or something. Now, it's gotta have crossed your mind that you're going to end up gay, like Rocky."

"Shut up!"

"Look at me, Cisco."

I walked away, heading for the bridge. Karen followed along behind me.

"It doesn't matter," she yelled after me.

I kept walking.

"It doesn't matter."

I turned around and stared at her. "So what if I told you it *does* matter? What if I told you it scares the shit out of me to think I might be like that? What if I told you it's the last thing I want to be?"

Karen came over to me. "Would it be so terrible if you were gay?"

"Yes," I said, not caring if I hurt her feelings. "Maybe it's okay for you. But it's not what I want."

She shook her head. "Cisco, you've gotta relax about this. You've gotta let yourself feel stuff."

I thought of Lara. I felt the softness of her lips when she leaned over and kissed me. I wanted to see her again. I felt that.

Karen stepped up and hugged me. "You're going to be okay about this, Cisco."

I relaxed into her hug. She kissed my cheek.

"I gotta go. I'm taking off with Alison Allingham." She smiled a secret little smile that betrayed mountains. "She's waiting for me."

"Alison Allingham?" I repeated.

"Yeah," Karen said. "Alison came home for Christmas. I ran into her at the tree–lighting ceremony downtown and the rest, shall we say, is history."

Alison Allingham. I never would have guessed. Alison was so smart her brain zapped people as they walked past. She sizzled with hyper intelligence, had graduated a year ago and was reputed to have won scholarships to every Ivy League school there was.

"Isn't she in college?" I asked.

"She decided she needed time off. For bad behaviour." Karen smiled, raised an eyebrow. "Anyway, we're goin' on a road trip. Should be interesting."

I resisted the urge to ask if I could go too. Instead I gave her a squeeze.

Karen flexed her biceps, punched me in the arm again. "Geez, Soames. You gotta start working out."

"Starting tomorrow," I lied cheerfully.

Karen laughed, then looked over her shoulder at the sound of an engine. A battered old Jeep clattered around the corner. She cocked her head, looked at me.

"Take it easy, okay?"

I scuffed my feet. Nodded. Karen started toward the Jeep.

Alison yelled out the window, "Hey there, Cisco!"

I raised my hand. "Alison," I said, then added, "You two have fun."

Alison laughed. I didn't know her well. But I can honestly say, I'd never seen her look so happy. Karen paused to toss a snowball at me, which I caught. Then she turned and walked away, giving me her backward wave.

I watched her climb into the Jeep, sling her arm over Alison's shoulder. I stared after them as they drove away. It took a minute before I moved, but when I did, I headed for the bridge. I thought about how I'd come here the day Rocky had told us that he was leaving.

"Fearful symmetry," as a poet I liked once wrote.

The river was frozen now. I dropped some rocks, trying to break through the ice, but they just bounced and slid farther away. I wanted to believe Karen was right, that it didn't matter. But the truth was, it did. I didn't want to be gay. I mean, who *wants* to be gay? If you have to wonder about these things, it's not a good sign. For the first time, I caught a glimmer of how Rocky might have felt and for some reason that really scared me. That might lead to all kinds of emotions—sticky, uncomfortable emotions I wanted no part of. I thought again of Lara.

I closed my eyes and tried to recall the night in the kitchen. I loosened just a little. I remembered liking the way she looked sitting in the moonlight. I liked her eyes and I liked hearing her voice.

If nothing else, I knew one thing.

I was going to see her again. I had to.

I headed home and grabbed the trusty portable from Delta's room, crossed the hall, kicked my bedroom door shut after me and sank down on the edge of my bed. I stared at the phone for five whole minutes, then punched in the number.

Lara answered. "Hey," she said. "Miss me already?"

"Lara, forget about March break. You come here for a visit. Now."

"You serious?"

"Yeah."

"I don't know if my parents would let me."

"Why not?"

"I've got school." She hesitated.

I imagined her scanning the checklist of handy ways to get rid of unwelcome geeks.

"I'm serious, Cisco. I can't just pick up and fly out there."

I couldn't speak. I had so much to say and couldn't think of a single place to start. I could practically hear the final *Jeopardy* music playing in my head.

Finally, Lara said, "You could say something, you know."

Like what? I know I'm a total loser? "Listen, Lara. Sorry I bothered you."

I hung up. My inner Steve Martin started with the loser jokes. I was unbelievably tired. I lay back on the bed and closed my eyes, letting myself sink into the white noise of chumphood. Old Mr. Patterson was having a field day, laughing away to himself in an upper corner of my room, just under a cobweb that hung there. The spider had moved house long ago and Mr. Patterson was plucking at the strands as if trying to provide suitably sombre string accompaniment to my black mood. I didn't hear the door open, or notice Uncle Vincent standing there until he spoke.

"Rejection," he said, "is part of life."

"So, it would seem, is eavesdropping," I commented, my eyes closed.

"Just trying to help, m'boy." Uncle Vincent settled himself on the Rocky chair. What was it with everyone? What pleasure did they get from watching me sleep?

"Do you mind?"

"Matter of fact, I do."

I sighed deeply. The mood music swelled from Mr. Patterson's corner. "So go on and get it over with. It's for my own good. I know. I know."

Silence. I cracked an eye to see if Uncle Vincent had gone, but he was still sitting there, observing me like I was a rare specimen of dogshit.

"Stop looking at me like that," I growled, and turned on my side.

The chair creaked and the side of my bed slumped as he sat down beside me. I curled into a ball. Sheesh. Couldn't anyone just take a hint?

"One of these days now, some day soon, I'd guess, everyone is going to get damn tired of this little performance, Cisco. You've had a rough year so far, I grant you that. But you gotta PERSEVERE!"

He reached over and shook me. Shook me! I swatted him away.

"Don't get all caught up in your own self-importance." Vincent was breathing down my neck now. "There's other people involved here. What about your mother?"

"Go away," I mumbled.

"For two cents I'd bash some sense into that noggin of yours," Vincent said as he left the room.

I rolled back into the centre of the bed. Mr. Patterson started shadow boxing.

"Go away, everyone," I added for good measure.

Last year, a girl hanged herself from a loading dock in the school parking lot. The grief counsellors were everywhere, hovering for days—just like Mr. Patterson, only real. I kept thinking, would she have done it if someone had smiled at her that morning? If someone had noticed sooner? My family was really into noticing, I had to give them that.

Right on cue, Rocky and Delta showed up next. No sooner had one train pulled out than another arrived.

"Cisco," Rocky said, "I want you to come to Stowe and spend the weekend with Ralph and me."

Looked like Rocky had given in to Ralph's idea that he should acclimatize the kid to the new living arrangements, like a plant you repot and bring inside in the winter.

"It's time you got to know Ralph. He wants to get to know you."

Think of your mother, echoed Uncle Vincent's voice.

It was hard to keep fighting. I think that's the first sign of going crazy—not caring.

"It's settled then," Rocky said, patting my shoulder.

Delta gave me a worried little frown. "You all right with that, Cisco?"

"Whatever," I said, sounding like some sort of stupid Valley girl. "Whatever."

23

I couldn't believe it. Somehow I'd allowed them to actually put me in a car and drive me to Stowe. Weekends at the ski hill were the busy time for Ralph, so it was clear that Rocky anticipated we'd have some quality father–son bonding time.

Their condo was precious, I'll give them that. Nestled in the mountain's elbow, it fairly dripped with yuppie charm. If anyone had told me six months ago—hell, if anyone had told me one month ago—that I would be facing an entire weekend alone in a gingerbread condo with my father and his boyfriend, I might have booked myself an ear-candling appointment.

Rocky showed me into the second bedroom, dropped my knapsack on the floor, gestured at the pine bed and pulled open the rustic curtains decorated chillingly with fifties-style skiers in tight-fitting stirrup pants. I followed him back into the living room, where a moosehead stared down at me from the wall over the fireplace. I swear, when Rocky turned his back, I caught it winking at me. There were little knick-knacks squirrelled away in the exposed beams. Rusted old ski poles. Equally rusted old leg-hold traps, looking as though a geriatric shark had happened by one night and forgotten his dentures. Someone had, in a fit of jocular irony, hung a birchbark quiver full of steel-tipped arrows from the moose's antlers as if to say, *take your best shot, big guy.*

"The place came furnished," Rocky said.

"That's a relief," I muttered.

Rocky gave me a small, resigned smile.

Ralph clattered around in the kitchen, then reappeared holding a plate with Wonder Bread fluffernut sandwiches perched like cottonballs in its centre.

"I'll make dinner," I announced as I skirted Ralph's proffered plate, avoided Rocky's eyes, and bobbed and weaved my way past the dreamcatchers that were hanging in every doorway between the bedroom and the front entrance.

Outside, I realized I had no idea where I was going. Not that this bothered me. After all, I hadn't known where I was going for quite some time now. I started walking. To halt the nasty little thoughts that were tunnelling away in my head like ants in an ant farm, I started humming to myself. Songs from Boy Scouts camp circa 1995. *Everybody haaaates me, noboddddy liiiiikes me, I'm gonna eat some wooooorrrrms! Great big juicy ones, itsy, bitsy slimy ones, I'm gonna eat some wooorrrms!* I switched to *There were rats, rats, with their baseball bats in the stoooore, in the stoooore! In the quartermaster stooore!* What sicko mind thinks of these kind of songs? I asked myself. I started analyzing all the songs I knew from camp and began to wonder if that's where all the troubles of youth start.

I made my way through a parking lot that was cheek-to-jowl with Range Rovers, Subarus and Hummers, pausing to wonder what the von Trapp family thought of the way things had turned out for a town that had started humbly on its road to fame after a group of apple-cheeked Austrians harmonized their way out of Nazi-occupied Austria and settled there. I read somewhere that there are people in this world who have seen *The Sound of Music* over 500 times. You'd think such folks might be happily institutionalized in an alpine aerie somewhere, yet the rumour is, they walk among us still.

Contemplating the life lesson presented by this disturbing thought, I entered the grocery store and began throwing the most exotic and expensive food items I could find into my shopping cart. I would make Rocky and Ralph pay bigtime for the pleasure of my company. Smoked trout, good-o. Gravlax at $50 a pound. I'll take two. Filets like burgundy velvet, perfect for something—stir-fried with a ginger/hoisin marinade and served with crispy noodles perhaps.

I carted the groceries back up the hill. The house was quiet when I let myself in—not even a tinkle of wind chimes. Rocky was sitting in front of the fire, his feet on a mushroom-shaped footstool, his hands resting on his shrinking paunch as he snored lightly in the late-afternoon gloom. He was exactly the same as he'd always been. Only completely different. It's one of life's constant mysteries that people conceal so much of themselves from the ones who are supposed to know them best. I made my way through the room carrying my bags, heaved them onto the butcher block and, suddenly at a loss as to what to do next, lay down in the middle of the kitchen floor and started to count the knots in the pine ceiling.

I guess I fell asleep, because the next thing I knew I could hear Rocky and Ralph in the next room. Obviously, they had no idea I'd returned, because otherwise they wouldn't have been talking with the unbridled vigour of a parent and stepparent debating the needs of one child versus another.

"I'm bringing the girls up here tomorrow," Ralph hissed. "My kids matter too, you know."

"I just want this weekend alone with him," Rocky said.

"He's got an attitude, that's for sure."

"It's been hard for him."

"It's been hard on everyone."

"All right, all right. Call the girls."

I sat up and cocked an ear. Angela and Sharon were joining us tomorrow? What about the twins? Why not invite the wives and have a reunion? Hell, why not call FOX and suggest a reality show? Call it *The Rocky Horror Family Hour.* I crept to the door, trying to hear more.

They had moved toward the window and were standing side by side, looking out over the snowy slopes. An acid pump in my gut jolted into high gear, corroding the lining of my stomach, killing my appetite. Rocky leaned slightly in Ralph's direction, Ralph put his hand on my father's arm. There are those who say at moments of stress that time slows down, but that's not how it was for me. Everything zoomed out of control. The anger that had been doing laps around my intestinal tract popped a wheelie and burned rubber for the esophagus. Throwing up was a very real possibility.

I'd never been into drugs, but I guessed I was tripping now; it was that surreal. Ralph murmured something and rested his head on my father's shoulder.

"What the hell do you think you're doing?" I screamed at them.

"Cisco!" Rocky jumped and pirouetted at the same time, coming down solidly on the edge of a rocking chair that started to rock uncontrollably, like it had suddenly been vacated by the ghost of normal. "Where have you been?"

"Right here!" I yelled at him. "Can't you see that?"

"Cisco, come here." Rocky started toward me.

His face was crumpled from where it had been pressed against the tweed of the chair. His hair stood wispily up in creative directions. Rocky. I stepped backward into the kitchen, hoping for some distance. There was a distinct fishy smell from where I'd forgotten my groceries and I got a perverse pleasure from thinking about all that expensive fish going bad. With no prompting whatsoever, my mind hopped, skipped and jumped over to another memory involving fish.

Rocky and I had gone whale watching once when I was twelve. The whole family had been on a trip to Seattle to attend a Grateful Dead concert. But after the week in a van and nights of five of us stuffed into a three-man tent, it was good to get out on the water. Delta and the twins had stayed behind, so it was just Rocky and me. The boating company didn't guarantee we'd see whales, but needless to say, I didn't believe them. I was sure we'd find one. After all, we were bumping over giant waves, soaked to the core, diligently scanning the foamy water searching for something that was ten tons in weight and the size of a small ocean liner. I mean, how could we miss something like that? Rocky's gayness suddenly seemed like that whale. How could we have missed it? How could he?

We never did see a whale that day. And we searched those waters for hours. Afterwards, when we were eating at a small restaurant just up the coast, an orca cruised into the bay and waved its tail, jauntily, as if to remind us all that we don't control everything. Especially whales. If there was a metaphor there, I really didn't want to think about it.

Rocky grabbed me now. He steered me toward the back door, snatching my parka on the way. He pulled me out of the house and down the path. When we reached the main street, he yanked me into a coffee shop. The interior was warm, and softly lit. Couples, families and kids were seated at just about every table. Rocky splurged for a giant foamy coffee, the kind he always says are a major rip-off, so I knew he had to be feeling pretty bad. A teenage boy and girl left their table and I grabbed it out from under a little old lady who'd been hovering nearby. She gave me an evil look but I ignored her. I decided I needed it more than she did. Mr. Patterson gave me a thumbs-up, as if he'd known all along that we were kindred spirits.

Welcome to Stowe, I told him, and he wafted over to a table filled with squalling children, ready, I guessed, to give them all a good scare, maybe levitate a latte or two. I tuned him out. I was getting better at that.

Rocky came back and plunked the world's biggest cup of coffee in front of me, paused as if toying with the idea of leaving me to drink it by myself, then sank into the chair opposite me.

I stared at him.

"I don't know what else to do, Cisco," Rocky said.

"Okay . . ."

He held up his hand. "I'm trying to break through. You aren't making it easy."

"Okay . . ."

"I wanted this weekend to be a chance for us to get to know each other on a different footing. I need us to try and reconnect."

"Well, sure," I muttered, taking a swig of my coffee. "I understand that."

"It doesn't look like you do."

"Do you have to touch him?" The thought checked out of my mouth like a guest that had stayed too long in a fleabag motel. Horrified, I stared at the foamy craters in my coffee cup.

"Yes."

It was that stark. He wasn't going to apologize. He wasn't going to back down, and so there we were. Exactly where, I wasn't sure. But we were certainly *there*.

I sipped the coffee. The machine behind the counter ground out one steamy concoction after another. Near the window, a group of cool kids my age had settled into the overstuffed chairs, looking like they were auditioning for the next hot teen TV show. A small dog, tethered to a lamppost on the sidewalk just outside the window, stood on its hind legs and stared in, living in hope that its master would be right back. I knew exactly how that felt.

"I think I better go home," I said.

Rocky's gaze wavered a bit. He seemed ready to challenge me, but in the end he just nodded. "If that's what you want. I'll drive you there tomorrow."

We headed back out into the cold. The streets were filled with winking red lights as cars transported people to their busy lives. I walked beside my father through the gloom toward the ski hill, toward the chalet. Toward the life he'd chosen over us.

24

It was after eight when I woke the next morning, having had an unusually good sleep. Unaccountably I was full of deep thoughts.

I had a pop-up video thing going on in my mind, where little off-camera remarks appeared in jaunty white boxes, pointing out the lack of understanding in my thought processes. It went something like this:

Roll camera: little boy at six years old trying like hell to build one of those papier mâché volcanoes that erupt when filled with a mixture of baking soda and vinegar. His face is proud, smeared with something dark like seaweed from the vegan sushi he'd choked down for lunch. Shining giant eyes, staring down the camera. No sound (Rocky hadn't figured out the audio part of the camera yet), just a little kid talking a mile a minute with no voice. Deep thought Pop-up: Kids never have a voice.

Roll camera: Same kid, slightly older, maybe seven, staying late after school, sitting at one of those pint-sized desks, running a slightly grubby finger (didn't anyone ever wash this kid?) under a line of words in a picture book. Nice teacher, my first love, Miss Agnelli, sitting beside me helping me read. Remedial reading class. Except I knew how to read perfectly, had since I was five. Read at a second-grade level when I entered school. Deep thought Pop-up: Pretending you don't get it gets you extra attention from helpful teachers. This preceded the Helen Keller phase by about four years.

Roll camera: Some sort of New Age gathering on the outskirts of Lovell. Billowy skirts that look like they are made from old sofa upholstery swirling around a kid with scabby knees and a head full of burrs. A lady with hairy armpits, hunkered down with the kid between her knees, picking the burrs out of the hair, painfully, one by one. Kid shrieking, New Agers passing by, smilingly like it's a cute scene. Hey! You think this is funny? Wonders where Delta and Rocky are and why they aren't picking the burrs out of the tangled strands. Deep thought Pop-up: You gotta have faith these people love you whether it looks that way or not.

The Cisco Show was just warming up, when someone knocked at my door, softly. They didn't wait for an answer; the door swung open with a tentative little *squeak*. You can imagine my surprise when I opened my eyes and saw Delta standing there.

"Rocky called me," she said.

I was confused. "To take me home?"

"Nope. Change of plans. We're all staying for the weekend. The twins came too. And Angela and Sharon. And Mona."

"Ralph's wife?"

Delta nodded. "We decided we all needed some healing and thought we should try and work it out as one big family."

Like I said, get the president of the FOX network on the line. The only one missing was Uncle Vincent.

Delta parked herself on the corner of the bed. "Get up now, Cisco. We all want some of your Belgian waffles for breakfast."

"Cisco," screeched the twins when they saw me.

So there we were. Just two great big, extended, angry families all sitting down to waffles, fresh O.J. and real java. Delta gingerly dipped a sickly green-tea bag in a cup of steaming water and watched the scene as Sharon, Angela and Mona stuffed the waffles into their mouths faster than I could pry them out of the waffle maker. Rocky and Ralph sipped espresso from demi-tasse cups decorated with drawings of coffee beans.

After breakfast I grabbed Angela and Sharon by their shoulders, pointed them in the direction of the dishwasher and grabbed my coat. Rocky started to get up, but Delta gestured at him to sit, then she shadowed me down the hall.

"Where are you going?" she asked.

"Don't know."

"Running away doesn't solve anything."

"Sticking around doesn't solve anything, since there's nothing to solve."

Delta gazed at me sadly. "Cisco—"

I could see her mustering up her sternest voice, the one she used when she really needed our attention.

"—this is getting so old."

I hate to admit it, but she did kind of get to me. Not enough to stop me from slamming the door and boot-surfing down the hill. I didn't fall, but it wasn't quite as much of an exit as I'd been aiming for, either.

I had a day to kill. I thought of hitching a ride back to Lovell, and filed it away for future reference. I'd start with a good look around town. Hadn't been to Stowe in years, and if this weekend was any indication, I probably wouldn't be back again anytime in the next millennium, so I decided to poke around for an hour or so, have coffee and watch the beautiful people go about their highly important beautiful business. Wondered how Karen and Alison were getting along out on the road to Los Angeles. Wished I had gone with them—chalked up another missed opportunity. Allowed myself to become deeply depressed, thinking how life would be so much simpler if I were only like Scarecrow in *The Wizard of Oz*. No brain.

There's a nifty little bookstore in the centre of town and I checked out the Philosophy shelves. I mean, why not? Couldn't hurt to get the advice of an expert or two. Of course, the store catered mainly to vacationing yuppies, so there were lots of espionage thrillers and self-help books. *Botox For Dummies*, that sort of thing. But I did find a book about Socrates and his six important questions. Wearily, I wondered what he had to say about this old life. So I slapped down a twenty, then headed for the nearest bar, fondly remembering the buzz I'd received from the wine I'd consumed with Lara. It was now about three o'clock and the afternoon was getting colder. Like I said, one of the advantages to being tall is that most times, people think I'm older than I am—a good thing when trying to buy illegal alcohol. Not that I'd ever bought illegal alcohol before, but today seemed like a good time to start.

I stuffed old Socrates ostentatiously under my arm, ordered a draft from a waitress who barely looked up, and headed for a nook beside the fireplace. There I cracked open the book and started to see if enlightenment was going to assist in forestalling my urge to tell the entire human race to piss off. Mr. Patterson must have picked up my vibe because he was there, amusing himself by tossing peanuts at the small children in the booth at the back while keeping an eye on me.

And so the afternoon passed. Sometime around four o'clock Mr. Patterson disappeared, circling around overhead with a great show of agitation before rising up the chimney in a puff of smoke. I watched him go, thinking that life might be kind of interesting in the next dimension if you could do tricks like that. Every time he disappeared I wondered if I'd seen the last of him, sure that sooner or later he was going to get tired of hanging around. I mean, this whole assignment had to be some kind of celestial *Fear Factor* for a misanthrope like Patterson. But, he reappeared moments later with another old dude dressed in what looked like a bedsheet. It took a minute, but it finally dawned on me. Mr. Patterson, bless his disembodied soul, was bringing in reinforcements.

I chuckled to myself, admiring Mr. P's enterprising nature, as the old dude, who looked like George Carlin, started turning the pages in my book and nodding as if pleased to see that he'd been quoted with some degree of accuracy. Under other circumstances, I might have found this highly annoying, but it's not every day your resident ghost conjures up a spiritual adviser with credentials like these, so I sat back and watched. The two of them had a fine time pointing and whispering and flying around, until Mr. Patterson, obviously tuckered out from his journey, settled down on the plastic spider plant for some shut-eye.

So there we were, just me and Socrates, duking it out for some kind of understanding on life's big questions. Like truth and happiness and stuff like that. Some of his thoughts on harmony got me, though. From what I could make out, harmony is adapting to change, cozying up to the universe, expanding as a person. It seemed like an awful lot of work and I wasn't at all sure I was up to the challenge. By the time happy hour had come and gone, I'd given up on Socrates and struck up a conversation with two guys around twenty with perfect tans, something that at the moment seemed far more important to success than achieving inner harmony.

"Wanna come to a party, man?" the blond one asked.

And I thought, why not? I had to muster an entire platoon of Dr. Philisms to fight off the fleet-footed gang of objections that came running from every part of my psyche, but with my new enlightenment—chiefly, adapt to the changes the universe sends your way—I beat back those pesky little insecurities, stared straight into his unfocused eyes and muttered, "Sure."

"Cool." He and his friend staggered slightly as they headed toward the door, and a pale shadow of concern yawned, stretched and suggested that I might want to rethink my decision to drive anywhere with these two, but I mistook this advice for negative thinking.

I followed them out to their Land Rover, wondering if this was what life was really all about, hanging with the *GQ* boys, cruising in overpriced, underperforming vehicles, looking like a poor relation, but again I shooed away this unworthy idea with a pep talk. You are a worthwhile human being. You have a right to be here. You have a right to be a hanger-on. No, delete that nasty little imposter. You are MR. COOL!

The Land Rover skidded out of the parking lot, fishtailed onto the snow-packed street and spun off into the night. It occurred to me that this wasn't the smartest thing I'd ever done, but I decided that it wasn't about being smart. It was about finding shit out.

They pulled to a stop about half a mile from a chalet that sparkled on the side of the mountain. "Look at the cars! This is going to be a great party!" the blonde one said. "Hey, I'm Max," he commented, turning to gaze at me as if he couldn't figure out how I'd gotten there.

"Cisco," I said.

"Cool." He nodded.

The driver turned slightly, showing me his perfect profile. "Judd," he said.

"Cisco," I repeated, then asked, "Who lives here?"

Judd laughed, "Ahh, who gives a shit?" He regarded me like he was wondering how I'd even thought of a question as lame as that. "Come on," he said, obviously deciding to swagger on, regardless of the loser he had unaccountably saddled himself with. "Looks like everyone in town heard about this shindig. Could be fun."

Max loped after him, while I sat there staring after their disappearing backs. So, that was that. My foray into the good life. I slumped down in the back seat, thinking maybe I'd just wait until they came back, but after about forty minutes my toes were so cold they had lost contact with reality. So I hauled myself out of the car and stamped up the trail, hoping to shake some feeling back into my extremities.

There were people everywhere. Some were outside puking, which was extremely amusing to watch. Inside, the air was filled with smoke and it was difficult to breathe. Someone had put on some horrible seventies disco music as if this was all a very big joke. I kept looking for Jett or Sam or whatever the hell they'd said their names were, but couldn't see anything through the haze. About six minutes into my tour of the chalet, I began to wonder if it was possible to get high from breathing second-hand smoke. There were bodies draped everywhere, girls in those midriff-baring tops and low-slung jeans that have cleavage on display at both ends. I would kill the twins if I ever caught them in outfits like that. It was thoughts like this, I realized, that were going to keep me from ever being a serious party animal.

I grabbed a beer from a tub of ice, twisted it open and settled on a couch, between two deeply stoned girls with matching ankle tattoos.

"We're best friends," the one on my right said tearily.

"But she hit on my guy," the other said.

"Did not," said the first.

"You are such a liar," said the second.

I fully expected a fight to break out, but they both started giggling and pointing.

"Liar," said the second one again, delighted at her wit.

"Bitch," said the first one. Peels of laughter.

They reached across me like I wasn't even there and started French-braiding each other's hair and insulting each other while laughing so hard they kept threatening they were going to pee their pants—which made me think it might be prudent to get off the couch and leave them to it.

Once I started walking, I realized I didn't have anywhere to go, so I kept on walking. Out the front door, into the snowy night, past the streets jammed with cars, back toward town. The walk cleared my head and I realized that I'd been gone a long time, since just after breakfast, and that Rocky and Delta were probably worried. I stopped. I couldn't walk all the way back to town, even if I knew which way to go. I turned around and headed back for the house. Guilt sizzled in my stomach like a drop of water on a hot grill. It was after 2 a.m. I stepped over a jumble of passed-out bodies, found a phone in the kitchen and dialled Ralph's number. The phone was picked up on the first ring.

"Hello?" said a familiar voice.

"Lara?"

"Cisco," she said. "Where are you?"

"What are you doing answering Ralph's phone?"

"I flew in last night," she said. "Your uncle called and convinced my Aunt Annie to let me come visit for a week. He met me at the airport and drove me up here. It was supposed to be a surprise. Where are you? Everyone's out looking for you. I'm watching the twins."

A chant rose in the background. "Cis-co, Cis-co, Cis-co."

"I screwed up," I said.

"Big time," Lara agreed. "Staying out all night is serious stuff."

"You're really here?" I asked, deciding to change the subject of how often and in how many ways I'd screwed up lately.

"Looks like it."

"I'm glad."

"I'm not so sure I am."

"Well, I don't care. I'm glad you're here."

"Thanks," she said. There was a smile in her voice.

"What do I do now?"

"I've got Ralph's cell phone number. Tell me where you are. I'll call him. He and Rocky will come and pick you up."

I gave her the address, then went outside to wait. Thought of a lot of things as I stared at the flickering stars. And then I started whistling. Mr. Patterson sailed in for the chorus, doing a fair impersonation of Jiminy Cricket warbling "When You Wish Upon a Star."

Forgive me if I tell you it brought a tear to my eye.

25

Rocky screeched into the driveway outside the chalet where I'd been sitting on the steps and amusing myself by running through the various ways I could explain why I'd run away. With Lara's appearance, it seemed terribly important that I at least look as if I had had some well-thought-out plan.

Rocky was out of the car before it had even skidded to a stop. "Cisco," he shouted, "what the hell did you think you were doing?"

"Sorry—" I began.

He held up his hand. "I don't even want to hear about it," he said, as if he hadn't just asked me to explain. "It's time for you to grow up. Do you have any idea what you've just put your mother through?"

Actually, I had a very good idea. One January when the twins were in second grade, they'd had the crazy idea—we discovered later—to walk home from school through the woods instead of through town, on their hands and knees.

They were pretending to be kittens, or so they said. Half the people on our street had been summoned to find them. Posses of neighbours roamed about, swishing flashlights back and forth. I'd thought I might dissolve like the Wicked Witch of the West, I was that worried.

So, yes, I do know what it feels like to be scared shitless. And, yes, I did feel bad that I'd done that to Rocky and Delta.

"Never mind," Rocky said, his voice shaky. "Just get in the car."

Ralph had watched our entire conversation from the front seat. He didn't speak to me when I got in the back and neither did Rocky. We made the trip back to the condo in utter silence.

That long-ago January, when, at around six o'clock, three hours after they were expected home, the twins finally crawled out of the forest, I'd been the one to find them.

"Meow!" Paris had squealed, staying in character.

"Ssssst!" India joined in, swatting at my leg with her paw.

"Jesus!" I yelled, jumping ten feet into the sky. I'd been so busy squinting into the treeline, scanning the forest, not even seeing the trees.

I was instantly on to what was happening. I hadn't spent three months as Helen Keller not to fully appreciate good role-playing.

"The entire town is looking for you," I screeched. We sat there for a minute, hugging each other as if we were about to be separated and sent by train to nasty places with Russian names.

The Jeep pulled up in front of the condo. "I'll leave you guys alone," Ralph muttered to Rocky as he climbed in behind the wheel. He brushed Rocky's cheek with his lips, and never had inner harmony seemed more like an impossible dream.

Delta, Uncle Vincent and the twins spilled out of the chalet.

I guessed Mona and the girls had already vacated. I looked over everyone's shoulders, hopefully. Delta caught the look. She reached for me, pulled my head toward her and rested her forehead against mine as if exerting some sort of divine-mother mind-control, then released me.

I found Lara in the kitchen, sipping coffee and listening to something on her headphones. I heard shh-ing and scuffling in the foyer behind me. I thought about retreating, but my escape route was filled with soldiers in the battle for my mental health, so I advanced. Lara removed her headphones and glanced at me. Her expression was amused and something else. Considering, perhaps? Doubtful?

Paris pushed me forward. Mr. Patterson started waving pompoms from his seat on the microwave as if he were in the bleachers at a varsity football game. The crowd cheered and I moved toward Lara while she sat and watched me.

26

"At last," she said.

I drank in the sight of her. She looked so refreshing sitting at the counter, dressed in skinny little jeans and a "Silicone-Free Zone" T-shirt. She'd cut her hair in the month since I'd seen her. It was spiked and black and made her look like a wayward pixie from the dark side.

"Hey."

She pointed at the seat beside her, and, doing my best John Wayne imitation, I moseyed on up to the bar. "Howdy, pilgrim," I drawled, settling myself beside her, pecking her on the cheek.

"Some night," she commented, completely ignoring my charming evasive tactics. She turned off her Discman, cutting the singer off in mid-howl.

The rest of the family shuffled in behind me. Paris and India draped themselves over the counter, taking in every detail of Lara's appearance.

"California must be so much fun," India said.

Delta settled herself in the breakfast nook. "Lara's been telling us all about living in Los Angeles," she said, as if it were perfectly reasonable for our family to be sitting around a decorator condo while Rocky's boyfriend circled the block and an exotic butterfly of a girl filled us in on life in O.C. The twins shoved soynuts across the counter in Lara's direction. There were bursts of conversation, but overall I'd have to say it was damn awkward. Rocky watched the driveway expectantly, waiting for the lights of the Jeep to reappear. Delta's face was an Etch-A-Sketch and each time Rocky jumped and pulled back the kitchen curtains it was as if someone had turned a knob and drawn a new worry-line between her eyebrows. Uncle Vincent leaned against the counter and watched the whole performance between sips of beer.

Lara yawned deeply. Her eyes were full of sympathy, but for whom I wasn't sure.

"Lara must be tired," Delta said, stating the obvious.

Lara nodded.

"We all are. It's been a tough night." She stared at me for a minute, then continued. "Let's all turn in."

She didn't have to say it twice. The room sprang to attention, and within what seemed like seconds, everyone was filed away in their appropriate places. Except, of course, for Rocky, who continued to sit and gaze out onto the empty driveway.

Sometime around 3 a.m., my door creaked open.

It was Lara, I realized with a shock, gliding toward the bed and, without even a whispered hello, pulling back the covers and climbing in beside me.

I resolutely stayed turned toward the wall. Lara kissed the back of my neck, and each and every hair follicle shivered.

"Cold," she said.

"Hmmm," I commented brilliantly.

"How're you feeling?"

"Let me get back to you on that one."

"Still upset about your dad?"

"Yep."

"What bothers you more? The fact that your parents are getting a divorce or the fact that he's gay?"

"Good question." I rolled over, found myself rubbing noses with her, like we were a couple of Inuit. "But I think it's the gay thing, actually."

Lara pecked me on the lips. "I can see how you'd be upset about that."

"Thanks," I said.

Lara went on. "You know, this kind of stuff happens more than you might think. Last year, one of my friends in California? Her mom left. Just like that. Moved in with her masseuse. Maya was so ticked she maxed out every credit card her parents had."

"Mall therapy." I nodded wisely.

Lara shrugged. "Whatever gets you through the night, I guess."

"Did it work?"

"Not really. She had to go to rehab."

"Rehab? What for?"

"Shopaholics."

"Is she all right now?"

"I think so. She's living on an island off the coast of Seattle with a guy she met in group."

"She gonna waste her life living in a commune with a guy she met in group therapy?"

Lara laughed. "Looks like you take after your father after all."

"What the hell does that mean?" I raised myself on my elbow and stared at her.

"You sound just like a guidance counsellor."

I tried to think of ways to keep the conversation going. It was very nice having her cuddled up to me in my bed and I was debating topics of conversation—things like the merits of organic vegetables, tattoo art or seriously original graffiti—and deciding none were quite what I was looking for, when we heard Ralph's Jeep pull into the driveway.

Lara sat up and swung her feet over the bed. "Looks like I better go."

She crept to the door, waggled her fingers and disappeared down the hall. I watched her vaporize into the night air and wondered if she was real or just some wisp of smoke that travelled the earth taking on the shape of a Dickensian waif and appearing wherever she was needed. I heard voices and realized Ralph and Rocky were having words. I slunk to the stairs, sat on the top one.

"So he's managed to scare off my family," Ralph said.

He and Rocky were standing in the living room. Rocky had perched on the arm of the sofa, his back was to me. Ralph was standing, facing the hallway. I could see the anger etched in every line in his face.

Rocky's spine was sickle shaped, as if it were bending under the pressure. I realized he was getting older, wouldn't be around forever. It was thoughts like that that scared me, because for the first time, I was actually feeling something other than total disgust for what he'd done. I mean, if you think about it, maybe Rocky had a point, not wanting to live a lie for his entire life. The thought unsettled me. It was a type of insight, some glimmer of understanding, and I didn't enjoy it one bit, began to regret I'd ever made old Socrates' acquaintance. If I let go of my anger, I realized, I might be in big trouble. I had no idea what might take its place.

"I'm sorry, Ralph," my father muttered. His voice was tired.

"Why don't I just go somewhere else for the rest of the weekend?" Ralph said.

Good idea, chirped a nasty little voice inside my head.

"I don't see how any of this is helping," Ralph continued.

"It's helping," Rocky insisted.

I bumped down one more step. The two of them had sat down. On the couch. I didn't want to watch, but I couldn't turn my head. Ralph put his arm around Rocky's shoulder and drew him toward him. Their voices dropped; I could no longer hear what they were saying. I debated letting loose with a primal scream, but like I said, for some reason it just wasn't in me any more. I reminded myself that there had to be room in the sorry old world for everyone. Said, yes, that is my father. Said, no, you are not the same as he is. Thanked Uncle Vincent for dragging Lara out here, for possibly saving my life. Thanked Socrates for making a house call, told him to send me a bill. Then I pushed myself to my feet. I had eavesdropped enough.

27

"Come see this cookbook," Lara yelled.

"I had no idea you were such a foodie," I commented as I took *101 Ways to Cook Venison* from her hand.

"I get into projects," she said. She swiped a hand through her picket fence of a haircut. "I like the idea of helping you plan some menus for your show."

"Steady on," I said, thinking James Bond would talk like that. The original James Bond, of course. "No need to overexcite yourself."

She gave me one of her baleful stares. "It would do you some serious good to get excited about something once in a while."

"Nothing will probably come of it," I said, checking out a recipe for venison with wild morels that sounded excellent.

Lara goosed me. She seemed to get quite a charge out of doing that, so I indulged her.

"I like a boy who can't get over his passive–aggressiveness," she said.

The twins barrelled over from the section on the occult. "We're going to start practising Wicca," India shrieked.

I glanced around the store, alarmed, then remembered we were in Vermont. No one even looked up.

Delta and Rocky appeared carrying a book on sixties music. Ralph waved his hand from the Alternative Lifestyles section and I forced myself to smile. The weekend was almost over. It was late Sunday afternoon; we were on our way to Lovell and back to real life. Uncle Vincent beeped. He was double-parked, waiting for everyone to make their choices. Just like Rocky had made his, my mind started to say, until I body-checked that thought into the boards. Even I was starting to get a little tired of myself.

We made our purchases and piled into the car. The twins yammered steadily and for once I didn't experience a single minute of annoyance. I watched the fields zip by, thought unaccountably about an ancient writer who lives somewhere in Vermont who still lives like it's the late 1800s. Takes all kinds, I realized, yet again. I started to read my cookbook. I had a lot of planning to do. Around noon, I'd finally gotten up the nerve to phone Cesare.

"Ceesco!" he'd shouted into the phone as if he had a bad connection, even though his voice was perfectly audible. "I'm stuck on the freeway. Damn L.A. traffic! Even on Sunday! Where are you?"

"In Stowe."

"Get my message?"

"I did."

"You still interested in this little proposition?"

"I could be."

"Playing hard-to-get?"

"No," I shouted as the phone suddenly cracked up.

"Whoa," Cesare yelled. "This crazy person just cut me off!"

"Maybe I should call back."

"Never! Here's the deal. I like your style. Moody, edgy. You got a thing going on. Kind of a Brando of Bison, I dunno. I want to do a test. Maybe get you to do some organic roaming the range—a kind of Wolfgang Puck meets *Dances with Wolves*. You ever see that movie, kid? So, anyway, we gotta move fast. I'll talk to your parents, see where we go from here. Listen to me. I gotta feeling we're on to something. Ciao." He hung up.

Lara watched from the window seat. "You going to do it?"

"Sure," I said, my head reeling. "Beats the hell out of staying in Lovell, now, doesn't it?"

She dipped her finger into a bowl of warm chocolate sauce. "I'll say one thing. You sure can cook."

Her finger now jabbed at the recipe I was reading. "Sounds good."

I grabbed her finger. I thought maybe it was possible that life can get better. I mean, if it can go bad all of a sudden, maybe it can be rescued, sort of like curdled Hollandaise.

Rocky and Ralph were following in Rocky's newly acquired second-hand car. We were a convoy of seriously warped personalities, just trying to get home alive. Uncle Vincent cranked up the radio and started wailing away with the song that filled the car. Even Delta chimed in, until we were all singing about getting along and thanking the great big universal consciousness for a little thing called *friends!*

28

"That is so cool," Paris said. We were all sitting around the kitchen table and she was shoving my homemade brioche into her mouth as if she hadn't eaten in weeks. Things were moving fast. We'd only been back from Stowe for three days, and Cesare had already booked me on a flight to the West Coast.

"Delta," India whined, "why can't anything exciting ever happen to us?"

I was scheduled to go on the same flight as Lara, and Uncle Vincent would be flying back with us. The TV pilot was scheduled to shoot by mid-February.

Delta closed her eyes and pressed the tips of her fingers against her temples.

Rocky pulled into the driveway. He was taking me, Lara and Uncle Vincent to the airport. Lara was sipping coffee with her eyes half closed.

Uncle Vincent swung into the room, grappling his duffle bag in one hand and his guitar in the other. "READY!" he announced as he parked himself at the table and reached for a brioche. "Delta, you sure you won't come to the airport?" he said between bites.

"No. You go ahead."

"It's sooo cool," Paris said again. "Your own cooking show."

"It's just a pilot," I said.

"Still," India groused. "Nothing good ever happens to us."

"Stop yer complainin'," Uncle Vincent said, staring at the twins. "Give your brother a break."

Delta pulled a thrift-store handkerchief out of her sleeve. Who knew you could even buy used handkerchiefs? She patted her nose and gulped some herbal tea.

Uncle Vincent reached for another brioche. "You going to make these for your pilot, Cisco?" he said.

"No. Cesare wants me to do a wild turkey with Rocky Mountain hazelnut stuffing for the pilot episode. It has a Thanksgiving theme."

"*Soames on the Range,*" said India. "That's such a cool name."

"Promise me you won't neglect your studies," Delta said.

Lara arched a brow at me over the steam from her cup.

The twins started bouncing on their chairs. "We want to go with Cisco, we want to go with Cisco."

"We'll go visit in the spring," Rocky said.

He was standing in the door, looking pretty much as he always had. Strange, I thought, how you think you know someone and then suddenly you don't. *Stop it!* Mr. Patterson commanded in my right ear. *Get over it already.* I was trying, but it was taking some getting used to.

"Hi, Rocky," Delta said. She patted the chair next to her. "Cisco made brioche. You've just got time for one before you have to go."

"I'll load up the car!" Uncle Vincent announced, pushing back from his seat. "Come on, girls! We'll have one last snowball fight." The twins followed him out the door, and Lara disappeared upstairs to grab her suitcase.

Rocky sat down. He rested his hand lightly on Delta's knee, and despite my new Socratric wisdom, I got an ache just below the breastbone. "Cisco," Delta said, "you don't know what this means to Vincent. Filming *Soames on the Range* at his ranch . . ." she paused. "Well, it could mean all the difference. The publicity and everything. I hope he gets to keep it."

"I do too," I said, glad for a change of subject. I couldn't imagine Uncle Vincent anywhere else. Truth was, helping Uncle Vincent with his money woes was one of the best reasons I could think for doing the show. That, and the chance to be a STAR, of course. Hell, I might even name a recipe in honour of Mr. P!

"Are you sure you feel up to this?"

"Delta," I said, "I haven't been this sure of anything for a long time."

"Virgil's going to help you?"

"Yeah. He's out of the hospital. Doing fine. He's going to be my assistant."

"Don't forget school," Delta said.

"You already reminded me."

"This TV thing may not work out, you know."

"Delta, chill. I know."

Rocky stood. "Time to go."

Delta gave me a long, teary hug. "Call when you get there."

The twins bombarded me with snowballs as I came out the front door. I looked around, realizing it would be summer before I was back. Maybe things would look different then. Maybe. No. Probably.

Rocky got in the car and revved the engine. Uncle Vincent folded himself into the front seat. Lara tripped lightly down the stairs after giving Delta a hug. I brushed the snow off my neck and pulled the twins toward me. "Take care of Delta, you guys." I kissed their cheeks, released them.

As the car pulled away, I saw them decapitating their snowman.

At the airport we checked the bags and then Uncle Vincent grabbed Lara and pulled one of his disappearing acts.

Rocky and I stood looking at each other. People rushed past, going in all directions, full of purpose. I could tell he wanted something from me. *Would it kill you?* whispered Mr. Patterson's shivery old voice from somewhere behind my left ear. An announcement came over the loudspeaker. Someone's cell phone went off, its "ring" the *William Tell* Overture. I tried to speak, discovered my words were stuck somewhere between my brain and my mouth. A flight attendant brushed by, pushing a small child in a wheelchair.

Go on, said the old voice.

I held out my hand. Rocky stared at it, looked at me, then put his hand out.

We shook.

He pulled me toward him. I felt his arms around me, smelled the sweat on his neck.

Go on, repeated the old voice.

I tightened my arms, held on. He gripped me back, I could feel some kind of tension leave his body. He pulled away, looked me in the eye.

"I love you, Cisco," he said.

"I love you too," I answered, trying to meet him partway.

We smiled at each other.

It was, I suppose, a start.

29

The plane lifted off and Lara grabbed my fingers. Uncle Vincent stared out the window like a kid who'd never flown before. Lara whispered, "You okay?"

I squeezed her hand. I was getting there. Definitely getting there. She stuck her headphones over her ears and closed her eyes. I concentrated on the good feelings, told the bad ones to take a hike, realized I'd finally figured out something important: I had that kind of power if I just gave myself a break. It was up to me now.

I guessed it always had been.

Which is kind of funny, if you think about it.

"What's so funny?" Lara asked, squinting at me like I was out of focus.

"Nothing," I said, kissing her lightly on the cheek. "And absolutely everything."

"You are so weird," she said.

"And proud of it," I replied jauntily, feeling like maybe, just maybe, I really meant it.

Acknowledgements

Like Cisco says, nothing can be done without help from friends, and in this case I have many to thank. First, I want to thank Matt (who happens to be a chef!) for all his insights into what it means to have a gay father and his willingness to share his feelings about his own sexuality when growing up. Thanks also to Kirk Munroe and Sergeant Mike Beatty for taking time to discuss some of the legal issues with me. Salaam to my agent, Hilary McMahon, who found a perfect home for this manuscript. And to Lynne Missen, my endlessly patient and insightful editor—thank you for making the book so much better! Finally, I do want to say that nothing would mean as much to me without my family—Terry, John, Daniel and Charlie—to share it all with.